P9-DND-029

Thurgood Marshall

Young Justice

Illustrated by Meryl Henderson

Thurgood Marshall

Young Justice

by Montrew Dunham

ALADDIN PAPERBACKS

To My Family

If you purchased this book without a cover you should be aware that this book is stolen property. It was reported as "unsold and destroyed" to the publisher and neither the author nor the publisher has received any payment for this "stripped book."

First Aladdin Paperbacks edition August 1998

Text copyright © 1998 by Montrew Dunham
Illustrations copyright © 1998 by Meryl Henderson

Aladdin Paperbacks
An imprint of Simon & Schuster
Children's Publishing Division
1230 Avenue of the Americas
New York, NY 10020

All rights reserved, including the right of
reproduction in whole or in part in any form.
Printed and bound in the United States of America
10 9 8 7

Library of Congress Cataloging-in-Publication Data
Dunham, Montrew.
Thurgood Marshall : young justice / by Montrew Dunham. —
1st Aladdin Paperbacks ed.
p.   cm. — (Childhood of famous Americans)
Summary: A biography emphasizing the childhood of the man who became
the first African-American to sit on the United States Supreme Court.
ISBN 0-689-82042-9 (pbk.)
1. Marshall, Thurgood, 1908–1993—Juvenile literature. 2. Judges—United
States—Biography—Juvenile literature. 3. United States Supreme Court—
Biography—Juvenile literature. 4. Civil rights workers—United States—
Biography—Juvenile literature.
[1. Marshall, Thurgood, 1908–1993—Childhood and youth. 2. Lawyers.
3. Judges. 4. Afro-Americans—Biography.] I. Title. II. Series: Childhood of
famous Americans series.
KF8745.M34D86   1998   347.73'2634—dc21
[b] 98-4080
CIP   AC

Illustrations

Contents

Other books by Montrew Dunham:

NEIL ARMSTRONG: YOUNG FLIER
MARGARET BOURKE-WHITE: YOUNG PHOTOGRAPHER
ROBERTO CLEMENTE: YOUNG BALL PLAYER
ABNER DOUBLEDAY: YOUNG BASEBALL PIONEER
LANGSTON HUGHES: YOUNG BLACK POET
MAHALIA JACKSON: YOUNG GOSPEL SINGER
JOHN MUIR: YOUNG NATURALIST

Thurgood Marshall

Young Justice

Naming Himself

Thurgood Marshall ran up the steps into his grandparents' grocery store on the corner of Dolphin and Division Streets. The afternoon sun slid in with him as he burst through the screen door calling "Grandma! Grandma Annie!" The store had a rich fragrance of fruits and vegetables. There were shiny red apples in baskets, big green cabbages in wooden boxes, pickles in big crocks, loaves of freshly baked bread, and peanut butter in a tub, which his grandmother scooped out into little wooden cartons for her customers.

And then he saw his grandmother standing behind the counter. Her brown eyes twinkled as she watched her grandson running into the store. "I'm right here looking at you!" she answered.

"Is Grandpa here?" he asked as he started to go toward the back room.

"No, he's gone down to the warehouse to bring back some more vegetables for tomorrow," Grandmother Annie Marshall replied. She looked at her grandson as he stopped and swung around to come over to the counter. She smiled with pride. He was such a fine-looking boy all dressed up in his school clothes, a tall seven-year-old. His dark pants and white shirt looked so crisp and neat.

Thurgood ran back behind the counter to his grandmother, and exclaimed excitedly, "Grandma! I've something to tell you!"

"Just a minute, Goody. Let me just finish taking care of Mrs. Reynolds, and then we can talk."

Thurgood was so eager to share his news that it was hard for him to wait to talk with his grandmother. He jumped up and down, first on one foot and then the other, as he watched Mrs. Reynolds selecting apples to put in her basket. She would pick up each apple, carefully twirl it in her hand, and then place it in her basket, or sometimes she would look at the apple carefully and then place it back on the fruit counter. He thought she would never finish!

Finally she finished selecting her apples and placed the basket on the counter with her other groceries. Grandma Annie went to the groceries, which were stacked on the counter, and asked, "Will this be all, Mrs. Reynolds?"

"I also need a ten-pound bag of cornmeal and a box of cornflakes," Mrs. Reynolds answered. "Then I think that's all for today."

"Goody, would you please reach Mrs. Reynolds a bag of cornmeal and bring it here."

He ran to the back of the store where the flour bags were stacked, grabbed the soft bag of cornmeal, and ran back to place it on the counter. Just then his grandmother took the reaching stick standing against the wall so that she could get the cornflakes box down from the high shelf. Quickly Thurgood said, "Grandma, I can do that!"

"That would be a big help," Grandma Annie answered as she handed the stick to him and then said, "I'll get started on making up Mrs. Reynolds's bill."

Thurgood was so pleased. He loved to use this reaching stick. Carefully he adjusted the handle and then balanced the stick so that the other end was right by the cornflakes box up high on the shelf. By a careful twist of the handle, the two little clamps opened and curved around the box, and when he tightened the handle, it was very simple to bring the box down. He carefully placed the box of cornflakes on the counter with the other groceries.

He was glad to see that his grandmother was almost finished as she touched each item lightly, writing down the price of each one on her sales slip. Then quickly she added the total of all the groceries. "That will be $12.78. Do you want to put this on your bill?"

Mrs. Reynolds nodded and said, "Yes, please."

Thurgood stood on one foot and then the other. He wished Mrs. Reynolds would hurry up; he wanted to talk to his grandmother.

"Thank you, Mrs. Reynolds," Grandma Annie said as she pulled out the wooden drawer where the accounts were kept and put the slip into the drawer.

Finally the customer gathered up her market basket and left the store as she said, "Good day, Mrs. Marshall."

"Now, come sit down beside me, and tell me what you want to tell me." Grandma Annie sat down in her rocking chair and motioned to Thurgood to come sit down on the big grocery carton beside her.

Thurgood took a deep breath and then announced in an excited voice, "My name isn't Thoroughgood anymore!"

Grandma stopped rocking. "What do you mean your name isn't Thoroughgood?" She looked straight at him and squinted her eyes as she added, "Your grandfather will be interested to know that. Your name is very special. You and your grandfather are the only ones with the name Thoroughgood in Baltimore, probably the only Thoroughgoods in the whole state of Maryland, maybe even the whole world!"

He leaped up from his box as he made his case, "But Grandma, Thoroughgood is such a long name to spell! So I decided at school today that from now on I will be Thurgood— Thurgood Marshall. I wrote it on my paper and I told my teacher." Thurgood stood up a little taller, pressed his lips together in a way that said "that was that."

His grandmother lifted her eyebrows a little and said, "Do your mother and father know about this?"

Thurgood hesitated as he answered, "I'll tell them tonight." Then he added with confidence, "And I'm sure they will think it is a good idea."

"Oh," Grandma Annie said. She got up from her chair and walked over to the back counter, where she reached down into the glass cookie jar, took out two cookies, and put them on a clean towel. Then she turned to the icebox to get a pitcher with milk, which she poured into a glass and placed on the counter.

Thurgood was anxious that she understand him. He followed her over to the counter and leaned over to help himself to the cookies and milk. "Grandma, I'm not really changing my name. . . . It is really only the spelling." And then hastily he went on. "You know when everyone says it sounds like

Thurgood. So I'm just spelling it that way."

"I think that's all right for you to change the spelling of your name. It *will* be easier, but you still need to talk to your mother and father about it."

Thurgood leaned on the counter as he munched on the chewy cookie. He wanted to make it right with his grandmother. He knew that he had been named for his grandfather Marshall, and he wanted her to understand it was just the spelling that he had changed. "You don't think Grandpa will mind, do you?"

Grandmother threw her head back and laughed. "No, I don't. You know he named himself! And I am sure it will be all right with him if you do the same."

"You mean his name wasn't Thoroughgood Marshall?" Thurgood was puzzled.

"His name was Marshall." Grandma hesitated only a moment as she went on to explain. "Marshall was a slave, and in those days, slaves often had only one name. He wanted to serve in the Union army during the war to free the slaves. When he signed up, the officer said he had to have a first name, and so he thought a bit and then said 'Thoroughgood.' He wanted to be good all the way through. So he named himself. I guess if you want to spell your name your own way, that's all right!"

"Did Grandpa get in the Union army?"

"He certainly did . . . and when the war was over, he joined the United States Merchant Marines."

"He wasn't a slave anymore?"

"That's right. After the war, there were no more slaves. He was a freeman, and he served as a sailor in the merchant marines for a long time. He worked hard and saved his money. When he came back to Baltimore, we got married and we used the money he had saved to start this grocery store."

The phone rang. "I need to get that. It'll be someone ordering groceries. You finish eating your cookies and drink your milk, and then I think it's time for you to run on home. Your mother will be wondering where you are."

Thurgood finished his cookie and drank the last of the cold milk, but he knew his mother would know where he had been. He stopped in his grandparents' grocery store almost every afternoon.

He ran until he came to the street where he lived with his father, mother, and his ten-year-old brother, Aubrey. His father had a good job as a dining car waiter on the Baltimore and Ohio Railroad, but he was gone sometimes for weeks at a time on the train. When he was on the New York-Washington run, he was gone only a few nights at a time, and Thurgood really liked that. Mother was a teacher, and she was always home after school.

Thurgood liked Baltimore. When he was little, the family had lived in New York

City and Mother had gone to Columbia University, but they moved back to Baltimore in 1913 when Thurgood was five years old.

He ran until he came to Druid Hill Avenue. He ran down the street past the row of trim brick houses, each with its own white stone steps leading up to the arch of the front door. When he came to his own house at number 1838 Druid Hill Avenue, he saw Aubrey playing ball with some of his friends on the other side of the street.

Aubrey called to him, "Where were you?"

"I stopped at the grocery store on my way home," he called back to Aubrey. Then he shoved the front door open and ran in, shouting, "Mother, I'm home!"

Mother was in the kitchen, just putting an apron on over her school clothes. Aubrey and Thurgood both went to Division Street School, the elementary school where their mother was a teacher. His mother laughed.

There was never any doubt when Thurgood was home!

He ran straight through the house, and started to go out the back door. "Can I go out to play?" Without waiting for his mother's answer he ran through the door and down the steps.

"Wait a minute!" Mother called after him. "If you are going out to the back alley to play you need to change your clothes!" Mother's voice was quiet but firm.

"Do I have to? I'm in a big hurry," Thurgood protested.

"Then you can be quick about it," Mother said softly.

Thurgood took off his shoes as he ran upstairs. He dropped his shoes in the corner of his room. He hopped out of his school clothes and threw them on the bed. He pulled on his old pants, and buttoned his shirt as he ran downstairs and out the back door again.

Mother came to the door. "No bare feet in the alley. Here, put these on." She tossed his old sneakers to him.

Thurgood hadn't wanted to take time to put on shoes, but he knew his mother was right. The kids were probably playing kick the can and that could be hard on the feet. He slipped into the sneakers as he ran to catch up with his friends in the dusty alley behind Al's house.

A Neighborhood Injustice

Mrs. Marshall was setting the table for dinner when she heard the front door open and Mr. Marshall came in. "Oh, Will, I'm so glad you're home. You're just in time for dinner." She went back to the cupboard to get another plate and silverware to set his place at the table. "I thought you might not be back until tomorrow."

Will Marshall took off his cap and hung it on the coatrack as he answered. "My run was shorter this time than I thought it would be. I'm glad to be home, too."

"You look worn out, Will," Mrs. Marshall said as she noticed the tired lines on his thin face.

"I'm exhausted. I'm away too much of the time. I would like to be home every night with my family."

"Oh, I wish you could be too. Aubrey and Goody miss you when you're gone on long trips."

"Where are the boys, Norma?"

"They are both outside. I was just about to call them," she replied.

"I'll call them," Mr. Marshall said as he stepped to the front door. "Aubrey! Goody! Time to come in."

When he went out on the front stoop, he saw Police Officer Army Matthews strolling up the sidewalk, swinging his nightstick easily as he walked. A white police officer, Army Matthews, patrolled the streets and the alleyways in their neighborhood. He always knew what was going on, and the people in the neighborhood knew he was always fair.

"Good evening," Officer Matthews said pleasantly. Then he said, "Aubrey is playing down the street and he'll hear your call. But if you want Thurgood, you'll have to call him out your back door because he's playing out there in the alley."

Mr. Marshall laughed. "I should have remembered. Aubrey plays with the quiet, well-mannered kids on Druid Hill Avenue . . . and Thurgood plays with the rough kids in the alley behind us!"

Aubrey came running down the street and in the front door, while Mr. Marshall went to the back door to call his younger son.

Thurgood and his friends were scuffling in the dusty alleyway. They had been playing hide-and-seek and had gone crawling through the old boxes and trash stacked along the alley. Al and Enoch were wrestling with each other as they argued about who could go first to get into the same box. Enoch landed flat on his stomach as Al gave him a shove. "Cut it out!" he protested.

Al said, "Quiet!" as he stood still and listened. "Isn't that your dad calling you?" he asked Thurgood.

"How come you got to go in now?" Enoch demanded.

"Well, you guys will be going home pretty soon," Thurgood replied as he crept out of the box where he had been holed up. He tried to brush off some of the dirt.

"No way! We'll be here for a long time. Come on back after you eat," Al replied. Then he said under his breath, "Not going to be anything to eat at my place tonight."

Thurgood frowned. "Where's your mom?"

"Down at the jail bailing my dad out."

"What did he do?"

Al shook his head. "Nothing . . . just on the street corner hanging out."

Mr. Marshall called again, "Goody! It's time to come! Now!"

"See you later," Thurgood yelled to his friends as he ran to his house and into the kitchen where his mother was putting the food on the table. His shirt was rumpled and his pants were dirty from playing in the dusty boxes and sliding in the dirt.

Mother looked at Thurgood as he started to sit down at the table by Aubrey. She looked out of the corner of her eyes at him and said, "Wait a minute! You need to wash your hands and face before you come to the table."

He ran to the sink, quickly soaped his hands and ran his hands over his face and then splashed the running water over his face and hands. Dripping, he reached for the towel and hurried in to his chair at the dinner table.

Mother had placed bowls of steaming hot soup at each of their places. As Thurgood sat down, Dad passed a piece of warm corn bread to each of them from the baking dish in the center of the table. Thurgood took a slab of butter from the butter plate, passed the dish to Aubrey, who also helped himself, and then passed it on to their father and mother. Thurgood put the butter on his corn bread and watched it melt into the little holes in the bread. He could hardly wait to take a bite!

Both boys were quiet, because they were so busy scooping the vegetable soup into their mouths and cramming in good corn bread.

Mr. Marshall told about his trip in from New York and how many important people were riding on the train to Washington, D.C. It had been a good trip. He was always pleased when there were so many diners in the dining car.

Thurgood was glad to see his father at home. Talk at the dinner table was always fun when his father was there. He would talk about what he had read in the newspaper, and he would ask Aubrey and Thurgood their opinions.

He also talked about the people in their family, and how courageous and independent their grandparents and great-grandparents had been. Thurgood especially liked to hear the story about their great-grandfather who had come from the Congo to America. He was one mean man!

"How was school today?" Will Marshall asked his older son.

Aubrey was a good student, and was proud to answer. "It was just fine."

"And you, Thurgood, how was your day at school?"

"It was okay." He was thoughtful for a moment. "I didn't get into any trouble." With a note of excitement in his voice he announced, "I changed my name at school today."

His father looked puzzled. "What do you mean you changed your name?"

"Well," Thurgood said slowly. "You know how long it is to spell Thoroughgood."

"And you are the only boy named Thoroughgood in the whole city of Baltimore."

"Yep, but I changed it to T-h-u-r-good today at school."

Mr. Marshall thought only a moment before he said, "It's a good idea . . . much easier to spell. Don't you agree, Norma?"

Mrs. Marshall answered, "Yes, I do! And I'm sure that would be all right with Grandpa Marshall. He's never been too careful about the spelling himself."

Thurgood spoke up quickly. "I told Grandma Annie, and she said she was sure it would be okay with Grandpa."

Aubrey added, "Mostly we call him Goody, so the way he spells his name won't change that!"

Thurgood grew thoughtful. "Dad, what happens when a man gets sent to jail?"

Mrs. Marshall and Mr. Marshall exchanged glances. They wondered what had happened that would have led Goody to ask this question.

"What do you mean?" Mr. Marshall asked. "Who do you know who's been to jail?"

Thurgood told him about Al's father.

Mrs. Marshall's narrow eyebrows raised slightly as her gaze met Mr. Marshall's eyes. He frowned a little as he said quietly, "I'm sorry to hear that."

Aubrey said, "Those alley kids are always in trouble. They never go to school!"

"Do so!" Thurgood shouted. "They do go to school!"

Mother didn't want to get into the argument, but she said softly, "I don't believe Al was in school today."

"Well, his dad was in jail . . . that's why, I bet."

Mother shook her head. "Yes, that's probably right."

"And Al said his dad wasn't doing nothing, just hanging on the street corner."

Mother corrected Thurgood. "His dad wasn't doing *anything*."

Aubrey said, "Maybe he stole something!"

"Did not!" Thurgood retorted.

"How do you know?"

Mr. Marshall said sadly, "Goody could be right, Aubrey. We don't know what happened . . . and unfortunately sometimes men get picked up and hauled off to jail just because they are in the wrong place at the wrong time, and *look* as if they may have done something wrong."

"I hope he gets out without any problem. Al's mother works hard. She doesn't need any more trouble," Mrs. Marshall said quietly.

Al's father *did* get out of jail. Thurgood wondered what happened, but he never knew.

Family Grand
Jury Member

Will Marshall worked for several years on the B & O Railroad. He was a very good waiter in the Pullman dining car on the train, but he was tired of being away from his family so often. When he had the opportunity to take a job as a waiter at the all-white Gibson Island Club on the Chesapeake, he was very pleased.

Not having to travel anymore, he had time to do many of the things he liked to do. He liked to read in the newspaper, *The Baltimore Sun*, about the trials and court cases at the courthouse. He liked visiting the courthouse and observing trials as they were going on. Although Mr. Marshall did not have a college education, he read a great deal and knew a lot about the justice system. Then when he was named to a grand jury, he was especially pleased. He was the first Negro[1] man to serve on a grand jury in Baltimore.

Aubrey and Thurgood were very interested in their father being on the grand jury. It seemed very important.

Thurgood didn't want to seem dumb, but he asked his father, "What do you do on a grand jury?"

"People who are named to a grand jury meet together and look at the case of an accused person to see whether there is enough evidence that the person has committed a crime

[1] Until the mid-sixties, "Negro" was a term used to describe African-Americans or blacks.

to press charges," his father answered.

"When will you be doing this?" Aubrey asked.

"I'll be going down to the courthouse tomorrow."

Each evening when their father came in from his day of serving on the grand jury, both boys bombarded him with questions. They wanted to know whether the grand jury had decided that some of the cases should go to trial. Thurgood asked, "What crimes did they do? Do you think they are guilty?"

Will Marshall was glad to talk about the justice system with his sons, but he told them that he couldn't discuss any of the cases. That was private information and a member of the grand jury could not tell anyone about a case.

One evening Mr. Marshall looked serious as he came in the house. They all sat down at the dinner table, but he was quiet. Mrs.

Marshall noticed that his forehead was drawn into a frown and he seemed to be thinking. He didn't answer when Aubrey asked him a question.

Finally Norma Marshall asked, "Will, is there something wrong?"

They were all surprised when he answered loudly, "Yes, there is!" And then he lowered his voice and went on slowly. He turned to his wife and asked her, "What do you think the first question is when a case is brought before the grand jury?"

Mrs. Marshall looked thoughtful as she answered, "I would guess, what crime has the person committed."

"The first question the jurors always ask is whether the person is white or black." He hesitated. "Today I objected. I said I thought the panel should not ask about a person's race before they make their decision."

"You're right! What did the white jurors say?" Mrs. Marshall asked.

"The white jury foreman agreed with me."

Thurgood's father felt some satisfaction that he had done the right thing, because never again during this session of this grand jury did the question of race come up.

One bright autumn day when Thurgood was ten, shortly after their father's tour with the grand jury was over, Mother asked Aubrey and Thurgood to go down to Grandpa and Grandma Marshall's grocery to pick up her grocery order. They brought their wagon and took turns pulling it. They had fun, running and getting the wagon going really fast.

When they got to the grocery store, they ran back to talk to their grandfather, Thoroughgood Marshall.

"So your mama wants you to bring her groceries home. You boys have your wagon?"

Grandma Annie was behind the counter taking care of one of their many customers.

She saw the boys and smiled at them, but she went ahead getting the groceries for the lady at the counter.

Grandpa was stacking up big baskets of potatoes, and he stopped for a moment and called over his shoulder to Grandma Annie, "Annie, did Norma call in her order?"

"Yes, she did. The list is over there by the cash register. I have most of the groceries she wants on the counter. You and the boys can finish getting the other things."

Thurgood ran over to get the list and Aubrey was right behind him. He tried to yank the paper out of Thurgood's hand. "Here, let me!"

"No, I got it first. I can get—" Thurgood pulled the list back and at the same time Aubrey grabbed it and between them they tore it.

"You don't even know where to start—" Thurgood started to say.

And Aubrey answered, "Of course I do. We need to look at the list and then see what's already on the counter."

Grandpa got up slowly from where he was working. "Give me the list." He went down the list, "Flour, sugar, baking powder, butter, eggs." As he read he deftly moved the packages on the counter from one side to the other. He muttered to himself but for the benefit of the boys, "Looks like Norma is going to be doing some baking." Then he looked at Thurgood, "All right, next on the list is a sack of potatoes. Can you manage that?"

"Sure," Thurgood said quickly, and ran over to the produce section. "How many, Grandpa?"

"Just get that smaller basket of potatoes." Then he turned to Aubrey. "You get two or three bunches of carrots, some beets, and a bag of those onions."

Grandpa, tall and slim, wore a heavy

apron. He walked over behind the register, totaled up all the groceries, and laid the paper slip in the drawer under the counter. "All right, now where is that wagon?"

"It's right by the front steps, Grandpa."

"Then maybe we'd better carry these things out and put them in the wagon." Grandpa handed the groceries to the boys as they came in and out carrying all the packages to the wagon. When they had taken everything out, Grandpa Marshall came and rearranged a few of the packages so the weight was balanced and the heavier groceries were on the bottom of the wagon.

"You boys get on home now. Your mama may be waiting for some of those groceries if she's planning on doing any baking today."

Aubrey started out pulling the wagon and Thurgood trailed behind, and then he ran on ahead. "Now it's my turn," shouted

Thurgood after they'd gone a little ways.

"You're not big enough—this wagon is really heavy."

"I am too! I'm ten years old!" retorted Thurgood.

"Big deal," Aubrey replied. He felt really grown up. After all, he was thirteen. He was turning to look at his brother when he turned too sharply. The wagon teetered and then tipped over with the groceries spilling out all over the sidewalk!

"That was pretty dumb!" Thurgood shouted. "If you had let me take my turn, it would not have happened!"

"If you hadn't been arguing with me, I wouldn't have turned the wagon so sharply," Aubrey shouted back.

"Oh, sure! It was *my* fault you weren't paying attention to where you were going!"

The two boys stood and glared at each other. Thurgood felt so angry that he punched Aubrey in the stomach. Aubrey clenched his jaw and swung back at Thurgood, hitting him in the chest.

Thurgood gasped. He had trouble catching his breath. Then he pulled back and really swung at his big brother.

Soon they were both flailing away with their fists, getting more and more angry as the blows landed. Finally Aubrey got Thurgood down on the ground and pounded him really hard.

"Stop! I give up!" Thurgood gasped as he tried to get his breath. He hurt everywhere.

Aubrey was sitting on top of his brother, one hand gripping Thurgood's shirt, and the other fist pulled back ready to pound him again. When Thurgood gave up, he dropped his fist. He was glad to stop the fight, too, as it was clear that he had won.

The boys got up and gathered the groceries. Potatoes were rolling everywhere. Thurgood picked up the sack of eggs, which was covered with the white and yellow of the eggs. He started to say, "Look what you did—probably most of the eggs are broken." And then he decided he'd better not.

Without a word, they finally got all the groceries back in the wagon and walked on home slowly, with Aubrey pulling the wagon very carefully.

Fighting Against Wrong, Not Each Other

When they reached home, Aubrey pulled the wagon around to the back door with Thurgood following. They each gathered up an armload of groceries and went into the kitchen. Their mother was standing at the sink, and their father was talking to her, saying, "I think I'll go down to the train station tomorrow, and maybe take the boys with me."

As Thurgood was putting his load of groceries on the table, he heard what his father was saying, and he started to smile with pleasure. Though his father didn't work on the trains anymore, he still liked to go down to see them at the station, and sometimes both Thurgood and Aubrey went along with him.

Their mother started to help them with the groceries when she noticed that Aubrey's face was smudged with dirt. And then she looked past him at Thurgood, and she saw his dirty clothes and torn shirt. Her pleasant smiling face became stern as she exclaimed, "What on earth has happened?"

Thurgood's heart fell. He knew they were in trouble. Their father turned quickly to look at them, and he could see that they were both dirty and disheveled. He immediately recognized the signs of a fight. "What is this?" he demanded. "Have you boys been fighting?"

Aubrey blurted, "He started it," pointing at

47

Thurgood. "He punched me in the stomach!"

"You are telling me that you were fighting with each other!"

Aubrey nodded, "But Goody started it. He hit me first!"

Their father's face was serious. His eyes were cold and he looked angry. He looked straight at Thurgood as he asked, "Why?"

"He called me names!" Thurgood retorted.

"You called me names first," Aubrey shouted.

"Well, you were stupid! You tipped over the wagon and spilled all the groceries."

Will Marshall stood up and looked squarely at his two sons. "Brothers don't fight with each other. Or call each other names. Do you understand me!" he demanded firmly.

Sheepishly, both boys nodded their heads.

"If someone else calls you names, that is something entirely different. I would expect you to defend yourself." Then their father said sternly, "Now sit down!"

Obediently Aubrey and Thurgood took their seats in the chairs at the table. Thurgood felt sad. He hoped his father wasn't so angry that he wouldn't take them to see the trains tomorrow.

Will Marshall stood at the end of the table. He looked straight at his two sons as he started to speak. "You have strong blood in your veins—fighting blood. But it's important for you to use your spirit and strength in the right way!"

He went on. "Do you remember the story of your great-great-grandfather who came from the Congo?"

Both boys nodded. Thurgood remembered the story well, but he wanted to hear his father tell the story again.

"Long ago, long before the Civil War, probably in the 1840s, a very wealthy man who was a big game hunter went to Africa. During the time he was in the Congo, a small black boy followed him around—"

Mother interrupted. "Some of our relatives said that young boy was from the Sierra Leone, a more civilized area than the Congo."

Their father smiled. "You know, Norma, that boy came from the depths of the Congo!"

"You are probably right," she agreed.

"Well, that's what Grandfather Williams always said." And their father continued. "When the rich man returned to Maryland, he brought the young boy with him as a slave. This small boy grew up into a big, strong man with a fighting spirit, who did not like being the property of the rich man."

"Life would have been very hard for him," Mother added. "He would have had to work long, weary hours in the fields. Slaves often worked from sunup to sundown, with a harsh boss leaning over them to make sure they didn't stop to rest. He would have slept in a rude cabin, with other men, and had very poor food to eat."

Will Marshall went on, "Back then, there were laws passed by the states, which forbid slaves to defend themselves against their master's unfair treatment. It was also against the law for anyone to teach a black person to read or write."

His eyes narrowed as he went on with the story. "This man who had come from the Congo became very angry at being treated as a slave, and so he became very mean. He did not want anyone to mistreat him.

"One day his owner came to him and said: 'You are so bad, I need to get rid of you. I can't shoot you, since I'm the one who brought you here. I don't dare sell you or give you away, because no one else would want you. The only thing I can do is give you your freedom. I want you off my place, out of the county, the state, and the country! I don't want to see you ever again!'"

Thurgood's eyes were bright with interest as he asked, "What happened?"

"That man settled down just a few miles down the road from his owner's plantation. He married, raised his family, and lived there the rest of his life, and nobody ever bothered him!"

"I don't understand slavery," Thurgood said.

Will Marshall explained how when the United States was founded, the white planters in the South needed workers to farm their lands, so they bought Negro men from Africa to do their work. And he continued to explain. "In the 1860s, when Abraham Lincoln was president, the United States fought a war between the states and the slaves were freed. Both of your grandfathers fought in that war. Nearly two hundred thousand Negro men fought with the Union army. After the war, as freemen, both your mother's father, Isaiah Olive Branch Williams, and my father, Thoroughgood Marshall, went to sea as sailors. Later, when they returned to

Baltimore, each of them started his own grocery store.

Norma Marshall looked at her two sons and said quietly but firmly, "You have courage and a fighting spirit, but it is important to use them in the right way. Fight against wrong, not each other."

The boys apologized to one another, and after they washed up they went out and sat down on the front stoop. Thurgood didn't say anything, which was unusual for him. Aubrey was silent, too. They just sat looking up and down the street.

After a half hour or so, their father came out of the front door on his way to work. He looked at Thurgood and then at Aubrey. He couldn't believe how quietly they were sitting.

"Do you boys want to walk down the block with me?"

"Sure," they both answered quickly, and hopped up to run down the steps.

Their father walked along briskly. "I need to hurry on to work at the Gibson Island Club now—and I won't be home until very late—but tomorrow is my day off—"

He didn't get a chance to finish, because Thurgood asked, though he was almost afraid to ask, "Can we go to see the trains tomorrow?"

"Perhaps, Goody. We'll see." He smiled to himself. He knew how eager Thurgood and Aubrey were to go, and he enjoyed seeing the trains almost as much as the boys.

An Incident After School

Thurgood awakened with a feeling of expectation. He opened his eyes slowly as he thought about what he was going to do today. And then he remembered. His dad was going to take Aubrey and him to the train station. He hopped out of bed. He hoped his father would take them. He ran downstairs, calling, "Mother! Mother! Where's Dad?"

Mother was at the ironing board, running the iron back and forth on one of Dad's white shirts. "Quiet, Goody! Your father's still resting. He worked very late last night."

"Are we going to the train station? Where's Aubrey?"

"One question at a time." Mother took the shirt off the end of the ironing board, put it on a hanger, and hung it on a rack. "The answer to the first question, I don't know. You will have to wait for your father to tell you. And question number two, Aubrey is reading a book in the sitting room."

Thurgood looked outside. It was a very gray, rainy day. He decided he might as well get dressed, so he would be ready in case they did get to go. The time went so slowly as he listened for his father's voice. He got a book, but he couldn't settle down to read. He started to go outside, but he was afraid he wouldn't hear his father.

Finally he heard his father's step on the stairs, and his low voice saying, "I think I'll go down to the railroad station. One of my friends, who is a conductor on the B & O Railroad, is coming in on his last run."

Then his mother asked, "Do you plan to take Aubrey and Thurgood with you?"

"If they'd like to go," Mr. Marshall said.

At this point, both boys ran into the room. He laughed, and said, "Okay, if you really want to go. Give me a few minutes to get something to eat, and then we'll go."

"What do you mean, 'last run'?" Thurgood asked.

"That's the last trip a railroad man makes. A man I worked with named John Anderson is retiring from his job. He has worked on the railroad as a conductor for many years. His trip from New York to Baltimore today is the last trip he will take as a conductor. This is his 'last run,' which makes it very special."

Thurgood and Aubrey loved to go down to the station to see the big trains chug in on their tracks, unloading their passengers at the gates.

58

Though the afternoon was still early, the day was darkened with clouds, and the rain drizzled down. The station was encircled with fog and the smell of lingering smoke.

They walked through the station and up to the tracks where the trains were stopped, having just arrived with their passengers, or the departing tracks where the trains were waiting to leave.

Thurgood looked at the signs posted at each of the entrances, listing the time of departure and the name of the destination of each train and the towns where it would stop on the way. He felt a surge of excitement as he looked at the names of all the interesting places the trains were going!

"Come," their father said as he led them through the gate and out onto the platform where the locomotives were standing. They stood beside one enormous, shiny black locomotive, which was huffing and puffing smoke from its smokestack up through the opening

in the roof above it. The smoke rolled up and just seemed to hang in the mist coming in through the roof opening.

Will Marshall was telling the boys about the locomotive with its big driver wheels and steam engine puffing away, when the engineer, sitting up in the cab, waved. "Hi, Will! Are those your sons?"

Marshall nodded proudly. Then the engineer shouted over the loud roar of the locomotive, "Mighty fine-looking boys!" And added, "Did you know John just made his last run today on this train?"

"Thought maybe I could see him," Marshall shouted back.

"Walk on down to the diner. I think maybe he's still there."

Aubrey and Thurgood followed their father as they walked down the platform. Thurgood looked at the big round steel wheels as they walked past the cars, and then up at the dusty windows. The train almost seemed like a thing alive with all its steam and smoke and noises. When they got to the dining car, their father swung up the steps and the boys climbed up behind him.

The conductor, John Anderson, was standing with his gloves, his lantern, and his rate book on the table beside him. When he saw Marshall, he exclaimed, "Will, glad to see you!"

"I wanted to wish you well, John," Thurgood's father replied.

Thurgood looked at the row of tables with their snowy white tablecloths.

John said, "While you're here, show the boys around."

Their father let them peek into the small kitchen of the dining car, and then they walked on through car after car. They marveled at the compartments where passengers could ride in privacy, and then at night their seats opened up into beds. They saw the sleeping cars, where there were narrow beds, almost like shelves. People slept behind curtains, some on the top berth and some on the bottom. And then in the last cars, they saw the coaches where people sat, and if they were on the train during the night, they just slept in their seats.

Their dad told them about the engineer who ran the train, and the fireman who kept the coal in the boiler to make the steam, which made those big driver wheels go around.

They jumped down off the train and walked along the platform, looking at all the locomotives waiting to go on their journeys. Thurgood wondered if John felt a little sad that this was his last trip. He thought about how great it would be to ride on a train and to hurtle down the railroad tracks going so fast. He looked up at his dad beside him, and wondered if he were sorry he didn't work on the trains anymore.

❖　❖　❖

The next day at school, when Thurgood was telling his friend Todd about seeing the trains, his teacher, Miss Smith, had to ask him to be quiet. He looked out the classroom door and saw his mother walking past with the boys and girls in her class following her.

"Thurgood, please turn around and pay attention to your work." His teacher was telling the class about Frederick Douglass, the famous black man who had escaped from slavery to become an important leader for African-Americans. Thurgood already knew about Frederick Douglass. His father had often talked to him and Aubrey about Douglass and his great work in helping African-Americans.

He spoke out without raising his hand. "Frederick Douglass learned to read and write, and he escaped from his master and went to New England."

The teacher sighed as she said, "That's

right, Thurgood, but I do wish you would raise your hand to be called on."

Miss Smith went on to tell the class how it was against the law at that time to teach a slave to read and write, so it was very unusual that Douglass was able to learn to read and write. She told how he became a speaker for the Antislavery Society in Massachusetts, and then later moved to Rochester, New York, where he published an antislavery newspaper called the *North Star.*

Thurgood was waving his hand wildly as Miss Smith was talking. Finally she called on him. "All right, Thurgood, what is it?"

"Frederick Douglass's house in Rochester was a station on the Underground Railroad, where he helped slaves escape to Canada."

"That's right. Can anyone tell me what the Underground Railroad was?" Miss Smith asked the class.

Again Thurgood spoke up. "It was the route slaves took to escape from their masters, and people helped them along the way to keep them safe. And the stations were just houses where people hid the slaves who were running away until they could get all the way to Canada where they would be free—"

"And safe." The teacher finished the sentence.

Thurgood added, "And Frederick Douglass came from Baltimore." Miss Smith shook her head. Thurgood was right, but he always had the last word. She took a deep breath, smoothed down her dress collar, and felt that her bar pin was straight. "All right, let's go to recess now."

At recess Thurgood told Todd more about the trains and locomotives. When they came back to their desks after recess, he drew a locomotive on paper and standing it up, made *choo, choo, choo* sounds softly and ran the locomotive into the back of Todd who sat in front of him.

Miss Smith looked directly at Thurgood.

"If you are not listening, at least do not disturb other people."

Thurgood didn't say anything, he just lowered his head and looked at his desk. For a short time he was quiet, and then he started to poke Todd in the back to get his attention.

Miss Smith walked down the aisle toward him. She was at the end of her patience. "Thurgood Marshall, that is enough! You go down to the principal's office!"

Thurgood closed his eyes and lowered his head. He really didn't want to go to the principal's office. His mother, who was teaching in the room down the hall, would know he was in trouble again. He hesitated a moment and thought Miss Smith might change her mind. But it didn't take long to know she hadn't!

"March, Thurgood. Right now!"

Thurgood stood up. He was big for his age and was almost as tall as his teacher. Slowly he walked out of the room. His classmates watched him leave, and they settled down to be very quiet.

He passed his mother's classroom quickly, hoping she hadn't seen him. He knew it didn't matter though, because the principal would tell her. He went into the office and sat down to wait for the principal to call him into his inner office.

Thurgood took a deep breath. He didn't really want to be in trouble, but it was hard not to act up in class. He got tired of just listening. The principal made him sit in his office for the rest of the day, and didn't dismiss him until after all the rest of the school was out.

Finally he hurried out of school, he was so glad to be free, and he didn't think his mother had seen him in the principal's office. He ran out of school and on down the walk in the warm sunshine. As he was running down the walk toward home he saw a group of boys gathered around his friend Isaac. He frowned as he tried to make out what was going on. They were calling Isaac names!

He hurried on to the group to hear some of the kids yelling, "Kike! Do you want to fight, kike?"

Isaac looked miserable, but he didn't do anything. He just stood there as though he were frozen in his tracks. Thurgood ran into the group swinging his fists as he shouted, "Go on, you dopes! Get out of here!"

The kids turned to see Thurgood, who was bigger than most of them, and they slowly walked away and wandered on down the street.

Thurgood scowled. "Isaac! Why did you let them call you names! Why didn't you fight?"

"What good would it do to fight?" Isaac hesitated and then asked Thurgood, "What would you do if they called you 'nigger'?"

Thurgood burst into the house a few minutes later, and with a frown on his face, ran back to where his father was sitting.

"What does 'kike' mean?" he asked.

Father frowned slightly as he poured the steaming coffee from the pot into his cup. "What do you mean?"

Thurgood was out of breath as he explained, "Isaac was just walking down the street, and a bunch of tough white kids started hitting him and calling him 'kike.'"

"What did you do?"

"I helped him run the kids off," Thurgood answered quickly. "They were no-good toughs!"

"I don't know exactly what 'kike' means, but I do know it is an insult—a put-down word, like 'nigger.' I am proud of you for helping Isaac. You were right in fighting for him; they had no right to call him 'kike,' just like no one has the right to call you 'nigger.' And if anyone ever calls you 'nigger,' you not only have my permission to fight, you've got my orders to fight!"

Grandma Annie
Takes a Stand

The late evening sunlight poured in across the floor, and the warm summer breezes stirred the lace curtains at the open windows. Thurgood's father was at his job at the Gibson Island Club, and his mother was sitting at her desk working on her lesson plan for her pupils.

"How much longer until we get out of school?" Thurgood asked.

She turned to look at Thurgood sprawled

on the floor with an open book before him. "Two weeks, Thurgood, and you need to work hard during these last two weeks."

Thurgood could hear some of the kids playing outside. "Why can't I go outside with Aubrey to play?" he complained.

Mother smiled, but her reply was firm. "It is important that you do well in school, and you need to read your lesson, because you didn't do it at school. Aubrey finished his schoolwork, and that's the reason he could go outside to play." She looked up at the clock on the wall and said, "It's time now for him to come in anyway."

At that moment Aunt Elizabeth tapped at the open front door and called, "May I come in?"

"Oh, do come in, Elizabeth. I was just going to get Aubrey. It's almost bedtime for the boys." Aubrey had seen Aunt Elizabeth walking up the steps, and he came in right behind her.

"It can't be bedtime, it isn't even dark!" Thurgood protested as he sat up and leaned against the couch.

"I know it doesn't seem right to have to go to bed when it's still so light. You may stay up for a while, since Aunt Elizabeth's here. But it is getting late, and you have to get up early for school. When school is out for the summer, then you can stay up later."

Thurgood was glad Aunt Elizabeth had come, and he put his book aside to listen to the conversation.

"Elizabeth, can I get you some tea?"

"No, thanks. I can't stay long, but I wanted to tell you about Mama. She's so angry!"

Aunt Elizabeth was Uncle Cyrus Marshall's wife, and they lived in an apartment on the third floor over Grandpa and Grandma's grocery store. Thurgood did not think he had ever seen Grandma Annie get really mad. Sometimes when she was annoyed, she would draw her eyebrows down and her mouth would look tight, but she never looked that way for very long.

"Angry! At what?" Thurgood's mother looked startled.

"Well." Aunt Elizabeth drew a deep breath and her mouth firmed into a straight line as she went on. "The Baltimore Gas and Electric Company was going to put a big power pole on the corner right in front of the folks' grocery store without even asking! The company man just came and started measuring and told Grandma Annie they'll be back to put the pole up tomorrow!"

Norma was sympathetic. "What did Grandpa Thoroughgood say?"

"He didn't have to say anything. Grandma Annie was furious! She told that company man straight out that was her sidewalk in front of her store, and it would be her decision how her sidewalk could be used! She flounced back into the store, but then she came out again and said she didn't want any old pole blocking the view of her store!"

"And so what happened?"

Both Thurgood and Aubrey were listening closely for Aunt Elizabeth to go on.

"Nothing more. The company man didn't pay any attention to Mama. He turned on his heel and left, saying, 'We'll be back tomorrow.'"

Norma shook her head. "What do you think will happen?"

"You know how those big companies are. They decide they're going to do something, they usually get it done, one way or another." Aunt Elizabeth looked disgusted.

"Is there anything Will and I can do to help?" Norma asked.

"I don't think so. I just wanted you to know what is going on." Then she added, "Mama is so riled up about this, it's hard to tell what she's going to do. But she's not about to let those company men bully her."

"I don't know what she can do," Mother

said, and then she smiled as she remarked, "You can't tell, though. Remember how she was with the census man?"

Aunt Elizabeth's serious face relaxed and she smiled too as she said, "That's right. That census man didn't get anywhere with Grandma Annie."

Thurgood was curious. "Who is the census man? And what did Grandma Annie do?"

"The government takes a count of all the people in the country and that's called the census. The census man comes to each house and asks how many people live there, their names, ages, and race," Mother explained.

And Aunt Elizabeth went on. "When the census man came to Grandma Annie's house and asked her the questions, she said she didn't know her real name, her age, her parents, or her race. All she knew was that she was raised by a Negro family in Virginia. You know how light her skin is, and the census man kept asking her whether she was white or black. She just repeated that all she knew was that she was raised by a Negro family in Virginia. And the census man finally gave up and went away."

The next day Thurgood could hardly wait for the end of the school day. When the teacher dismissed the class, he ran down the steps of school and hurried on to his grandparents' grocery store. When he was almost there he saw Grandma Annie sitting in her straight kitchen chair on the sidewalk right in front of the store!

"Grandma! Grandma!" he shouted as he came up to her. "Why are you sitting out here?"

She looked at him and answered calmly, just as if she always sat out in the middle of the sidewalk. "Well, the electric company men think they are going to put a pole here. It's my sidewalk and I don't want a pole here." She smiled pleasantly. "Your grandfather is inside, go on in. I think he can find a cookie or two for you."

Aubrey came running up just then, and they both went inside where Grandpa Marshall greeted them. "Come on, boys. Here's a couple of your grandmother's cookies." He chuckled. "She's a little busy right now."

"Why is she sitting out there on the sidewalk?" Aubrey asked.

"The electric company came to put up their pole, and she just took her kitchen chair and sat down where they were fixing to make the hole to set it in. The workmen talked and talked to her trying to get her to move. Then they went and got the big boss. He came and he talked and talked. Grandma didn't say anything. She just sat there."

Three days later Enoch ran up to Thurgood as they were walking home from school and said, "How come your grandma is sitting out there on the sidewalk in front of the grocery store? She's been out there every day."

Thurgood answered, "She isn't going to let the electric company put a big pole on the sidewalk in front of the grocery store."

Enoch said, "She can't keep them from it, can she? When the electric company wants to put in a pole, they put in a pole." He hesitated and then said, "Don't they?"

Thurgood shrugged. "I don't know. But you don't know my grandma when she makes up her mind."

That evening Thurgood asked his mother and dad, "Everybody's talking about Grandma Annie sitting on the sidewalk. How long is she going to sit there?"

His dad answered, "I expect as long as she needs to."

The next day when Thurgood went past the grocery store, Grandma was still sitting very calmly on her chair. She smiled and told Thurgood to go on in the store. Grandpa was taking care of their customers, but he looked out at his wife sitting there on her sidewalk.

"They said they're coming back tomorrow with a paper from the court to make her move."

Thurgood asked, "Can they do that?"

"They can do whatever they want, but they aren't going to move Grandma once she makes up her mind!"

And Grandpa Marshall was right!

The electric company people came back day after day. They threatened. They cajoled. They brought court papers, but still Grandma Annie didn't move.

Finally, the Baltimore Gas and Electric Company put their pole up at another location around the corner, and Grandma Annie took her kitchen chair and went back inside her grocery store.

All of the Marshall family were proud of Annie Marshall and how she had stood up for her rights, and won!

Visiting the Courthouse

Though the morning was still early, the sun was high in the sky and the air in the house was heavy and hot. Mrs. Marshall was washing the breakfast dishes, when Mr. Marshall stepped into the kitchen and said, "Norma, I think I'll go down to the courthouse today."

She nodded. She had thought that he might spend his day off from work going down to the courthouse to visit some of the courtrooms. At that moment Thurgood came rushing in. Both his parents looked up as the screen door slammed behind him. He was so hot that his shirt was wet with sweat, and droplets of perspiration ran down his face. "I need a drink of water," he announced as he went to the sink and grabbed a glass.

"I'm going down to the courthouse. Would you like to go with me?" his father asked.

Thurgood answered without hesitation. "Sure." He felt lucky that he had come into the house at just the right time.

"Wash your face, Thurgood," his mother said, "and go change your shirt."

Will Marshall liked to go down to the courthouse to visit the courtrooms when trials were in session, and often he would take Thurgood with him. They rode the trolley together down to the courthouse. Thurgood felt like he was walking into a very special place as he strode up the steps to the big building. The corridors were wide and dark, flanked by big wooden doors. There was a special smell of waxed wooden floors and warm, stale air. Quietly they walked into one large courtroom, where a jury was being selected. There were so many people, Thurgood could not understand exactly what was happening. His father whispered to him that all the people sitting in the audience section had been called to serve on the jury for a trial.

Thurgood whispered, "All those people? I thought there were only twelve people on a jury."

"That's right. The lawyers choose just twelve people from all those people who have been called. The rest will leave."

They sat for a short while and watched as the lawyers questioned one person after another, and most of the people questioned then left. Only three of the people questioned went to the seats in the jury box.

"Come, let's go." His father stood up. After they went through the doors into the corridor he said, "That was going to take a very long time."

"Why?" Thurgood asked. He was puzzled. "Why did they send so many people away?"

"The lawyers for both sides ask questions of each person to try to select people who will be fair on the jury. If a person has an attitude or knows something that might cause that person to be unfair, the lawyers will not choose him or her."

They walked on down the corridor to another courtroom. Quietly they walked in through the heavy wooden doors. They sat down in the back of the room. The ceiling fans were whirring and hot summer breezes floated in the open windows.

Two of the lawyers were standing at the judge's bench. They were talking softly with each other and with the judge. Thurgood tried to listen, but he couldn't hear anything they were saying. He asked his father, "What are they doing?"

His father whispered very quietly, "I don't know, but lawyers sometimes talk to the judge like that about things they don't want the jury to hear."

Thurgood looked at the people who were sitting in the jury box. They looked like just everyday white folks. He wondered what they were thinking.

Soon the lawyers returned, each to his own table, and the trial continued. The defendant was accused of armed robbery. Thurgood sat up straight so he could see past the people in front of him. At first he could see only the back of the accused man. The man who was accusing him was a white man who owned a drug store that had been robbed.

As the prosecuting attorney asked the questions, the drugstore man said that the robber had come in with a gun, pointed it at him, and took all the money in the cash drawer. The attorney asked, "Can you identify the man?"

And the accuser said, "I sure can. That's him right there!" And he pointed his finger at the slim dark man who was the defendant. Thurgood could see the defendant's shoulders droop.

Then when it was the defendant's turn to be questioned, his lawyer, a young, athletic-looking white man asked, "Jeremiah, do you have a gun?"

"No, sir, I don't."

And then, "Where were you the night of February 22?"

"I think I was at home," the defendant answered uncertainly.

"You don't know where you were?" his lawyer asked.

"I just know where I was not!" Jeremiah raised his voice as he said, "I was not at that man's store!"

When the prosecutor questioned him, he shot questions at him one after another, and finally with his voice raised, "And if you don't own a gun, where did you get the gun!"

Thurgood couldn't help feeling sorry for the poor man on the stand, who answered weakly in a soft voice, "I did not have no gun." It was almost as if he knew that he was going to be judged guilty.

And he was. The people in the jury all filed out and in a very short time returned to the jury box. The jury foreman stood and announced the verdict of guilty, and then the judge set the sentence of ten years in prison.

Thurgood felt troubled as they walked out of the courtroom. He didn't know how the people in the jury could really know that Jeremiah was guilty. And how had they decided so quickly? Thurgood was unusually quiet as he rode home on the trolley.

At dinner Mother put out the platter of fried chicken, with mashed potatoes and gravy, fresh green beans, and sliced tomatoes and cucumbers, served with a big loaf of baked bread from her folks' grocery store. They all ate hungrily, and there was little conversation as they all enjoyed the good food. Aubrey and Thurgood were both hungry. They were always hungry!

Finally when Thurgood had cleaned his plate, and was still chewing on a drumstick until the bone was licked clean, he asked his father, "Do you think that man really robbed that drugstore?"

Thurgood laid the bone down on his plate. He frowned as he thought about that man going to jail. He had an uneasy feeling that things were not quite right, and he needed to talk about it.

"What man?" Aubrey asked. "What are you talking about?"

Will Marshall didn't answer Aubrey, but turned to Thurgood, and asked, "What do you think?"

"I felt sorry for him."

"But that doesn't answer the question. You

could feel sorry for him whether he was the robber or not. Do you think he was the robber?"

Aubrey interrupted. "What are you talking about? What robber?"

"Your father and Thurgood went down to the courthouse this afternoon, and this was one of the trials that they saw," Mother explained.

"You went to the courthouse! How come I didn't get to go?" demanded Aubrey.

"Aubrey," Mother said in her no-nonsense voice, "you weren't home when they got ready to go, so you didn't get to go. You go often enough with your father and Thurgood."

Will Marshall turned to Thurgood and asked again, "Was he guilty, or not?"

Thurgood puzzled for a moment. He narrowed his eyes as he thought. He answered slowly, "I guess I don't know for sure, but I don't think they proved he had a gun, and I don't think they proved he was there!"

"But he could not prove he was *not* there!" his father answered.

"And he said he didn't have a gun!" Thurgood added.

"He could have just said that," Aubrey argued. "He might have been lying."

"He was on the stand. He *had* to tell the truth," Thurgood said slowly. Then he frowned as he blurted out, "He had sworn to tell the truth!"

"Thurgood, you are right." Then his father said softly, "Do you suppose sometimes a person might be tempted to lie if telling the truth would get him into more trouble?"

Thurgood shook his head as he pushed back from the table.

"He had a lawyer appointed by the court, and a trial by jury," Thurgood's father said. "Though I agree that his lawyer was a young public defender, who didn't seem to help Jeremiah's case too much."

"But all those people were white, and he was a Negro. If he had a jury with Negroes on it, they might have understood better."

Will Marshall's mouth grew tight under his bushy mustache. "Thurgood, you are right, but not many Negroes get picked for a jury."

Thurgood stood up and said loudly, "I don't think he was guilty!"

"Sit down, Thurgood. I agree with you. To judge a man guilty of a crime, it is the burden of the state to prove the case beyond a reasonable doubt. The prosecuting attorney certainly did not prove the case beyond a reasonable doubt! I agree with you. I don't think that man received justice either."

Mother thought how many times it seemed that poor, uneducated people did not seem to be treated fairly. She looked at her two sons and said firmly, "It is very important that you both get a good education so that you can do well. Aubrey, you're doing so well in high school and you'll be going to college when you graduate."

Aubrey spoke up, "I want to be a doctor when I grow up."

"That's a good choice," Mother agreed. "You're a very good student in your science courses, and I'm sure you will do well in medical school. It's a long, difficult course of study, but you can be sure that your father and I will help you."

Mother half smiled as she turned to Thurgood. "You need a good education too, but first you need to pay more attention in class and less time in the principal's office." Then she added, "What do you think you would like to be?"

Thurgood shrugged his shoulders. "I don't know."

Mother said, "Well, I think you would be a good dentist. Negro doctors and dentists are very successful."

Corn Bread and Deep Thoughts

Thurgood jammed his hands down into his pants pockets as he walked down the street to his grandparents Williams, who were his mother's parents. Grandma Mary Eliza had told him to come on over for supper and that she wanted to send something home with him. Often Grandma Mary Eliza baked bread or cookies for her children and grandchildren.

Thurgood whistled as he walked along.

The big trees made shady patterns of their leaves and branches on the sidewalk in the warm sunshine. He thought about how soon school would be out for the summer. He counted up the days. There would be the rest of this week—that would be three days—and then all the next week. Friday really wouldn't count because that would be graduation day. So that meant there were only seven more days of school! He could hardly believe that he was going to graduate from eighth grade!

Then he thought about going to high school in September. After summer was over he would be going to Frederick Douglass High School with his brother. Aubrey would be a senior and knew that he wanted to be a doctor. Thurgood didn't know what he wanted to be. He whistled some as he thought. He tried to imagine being a dentist, but he just didn't know.

He did feel a twinge of uneasiness about going to high school. Though he often got into trouble at Division Street Elementary School, he knew his way around. All the teachers knew him. Then he laughed as he thought, maybe they knew him too well because he spent so much time in the principal's office.

As he walked along, he passed the big brick school where the white kids went. He looked at the smooth asphalt play yard. There were some kids playing basketball at the shiny big basketball hoops with their white nets. There was also a big area with playground equipment where some younger kids were laughing and playing.

He walked a little more slowly as he thought about the dusty dirt playground they had at Division Street School, and the old brick building where they went to school. He knew that he and Aubrey went to schools that were attended only by Negro children. The white kids went to different schools. Even Isaac who lived on his block went to a different school. It made him feel kind of mad. The white kids walked past his house every day to go to their school, and he walked right past that big fine school to go on to his school.

He didn't understand. He thought about where they lived. Baltimore really wasn't a southern city. They could sit any place they wanted on the trolleys, and he knew that in some southern cities, Negroes could sit only in the back of the trolley. And yet, he jammed his hands deeper in his pockets and frowned as he thought, *Why were there different schools for whites and Negroes?* And then he kept on thinking about how things were in Baltimore: separate toilets for White and Colored, separate drinking fountains for White and Colored, and even restaurants with two doors, one for White and one for Colored. He didn't understand.

He ran up the sidewalk toward his grandparents' house. He passed their next-door neighbor, a tall, skinny white man, standing with a shovel by the fence between the two houses. "Hi," Thurgood called as he walked past.

The neighbor just looked over his shoulder and didn't answer. He just said, "Harrumph," in a very cross tone.

Thurgood just shrugged and ran on up to his grandparents' front porch and knocked on the screen door. The flies were buzzing around. "Come on in. Is that you, Goody?" Grandma called from the kitchen.

Thurgood ran in quickly so the flies didn't come with him. "Hi, Grandma. Is Grandpa Isaiah Olive Branch Williams here?"

He loved to roll his grandfather's name off his tongue. Both of his grandfathers had the most special names!

Grandma laughed. "No, he isn't, Goody. Grandpa is down at the store, but he'll be home very soon."

Thurgood was quiet for a moment as he thought, and then he said slowly, "Seems funny that both my grandparents have grocery stores."

"Oh, not so funny," Grandma answered quickly. "Everyone needs to buy groceries. It's a good business. Isaiah went to sea with the United States Merchant Marines. He saved his money, and when he came back to Baltimore, he took the money he had saved and went into the grocery business. Your other grandfather, Thoroughgood Marshall, went to sea too, and he did exactly the same thing. Our stores are far enough apart that there are plenty of customers for both of us," Grandma explained.

Thurgood sat down at the kitchen table, propped his chin on his hands as he said, "Maybe I'll go to sea and then get a grocery store."

Grandma threw her head back and laughed merrily. "I think your folks have other plans for you. You need to get a good education!"

Thurgood nodded. "I know. My mama thinks I should be a dentist."

"Is that what you think you'd like to do?" Grandma asked.

Thurgood drew his eyebrows together in a frown. "I don't know, and I think I need to decide. I'm going to high school in September."

Grandmother stood up straight and tall, and smoothed down her apron as she said, "I agree with your parents that you need a good education, but you also need to learn to cook. No one ever heard of a cook going hungry. Cooks can always get jobs!"

With that she got the bag of cornmeal out of the cupboard and set it on the table with a thud. "Thurgood, roll up your sleeves and wash your hands. We're going to make corn bread!"

She struck a kitchen match, and as the wooden match flared into an orange flame, she turned on the gas in the oven and put the match in. The oven caught the flame with a *poof*, and Grandma closed the oven door. "We need a nice hot oven." And then she said, "Now we need a good-size mixing bowl." She placed a large crockery bowl on the table and directed Thurgood, "Get three pans out of the pantry. We'll make corn bread for your folks, one for Uncle Fearless, and one for Grandpa and me."

He got three pans out of the pantry and lined them up on the table. Then he untied the string from around the top of the bag of cornmeal. He lifted the bag, and holding the bottom with one hand, he poured the golden cornmeal into the bowl. "Tell me when to stop, Grandma."

Her dark eyes squinted as she looked through her glasses at the bowl. "Put in just a little more. Fill the bowl to about here," and she placed her index finger at the side of the bowl about three inches from the top.

"Okay, what do I do next?"

Grandma got out the baking powder and salt and told Thurgood to put them into the cornmeal and stir the dry mixture with a large wooden spoon. "And now we'll put in some sugar."

"Is there sugar in corn bread?" Thurgood asked.

"Sugar in corn bread!" Grandma chuckled. "There is in *my* corn bread! Some people make corn bread without sugar but not me. And my corn bread never goes begging!"

And Thurgood knew what she meant. Everyone always liked Grandma Mary Eliza's corn bread. "Now what?" he asked as he waved his spoon in the air scattering some of the dry cornmeal on the table and on the floor.

"Thoroughgood! Keep that spoon in the bowl!" Grandma scolded, and then she turned to the stove. "First, I need to check the oven." She opened the oven door and with her hand felt the heat of the oven. "I think the oven needs to be a little hotter." She adjusted the oven key a little. "There, that will be just right when we put the batter into the oven." She went to the wooden icebox and got out a large pitcher of milk.

"Can I pour it in?" asked Thurgood eagerly.

"Yes, but do it slowly."

Thurgood took the pitcher and started to pour the creamy milk into the bowl of dry ingredients. "How much do I put in?"

"Oh, just about as much as a person would drink," Grandma answered. "I think that's about enough." She took the pitcher from Thurgood. "Now stir all the milk in with the cornmeal."

Thurgood stirred slowly until the mixture was all smooth. Grandma went to the stove top where a big kettle of soup was simmering. "Can I help you make the soup, Grandma?"

"Next time, Goody. I do want you to learn to cook a good pot of soup, but this soup is just about done. It just needs to cook a little longer."

"Is this stirred enough?"

Grandma took the spoon from Thurgood and turned it through the smooth batter. "Looks good. We need to add the eggs." She got the eggs out of the bowl in the ice-box, and laid them on the table by Thurgood. He picked them up one at a time, and cracked the shells on the edge of the mixing bowl. Then holding a shell in each hand, he poured the liquid egg into the batter. "Stir the eggs in nice and smooth, and then we have just one more thing." She took a can of bacon drippings from the back of the stove top and poured a little into the batter.

The little puddle of oil settled on the top of the yellow mixture. "Just take a couple turns of your spoon to run that all through the corn bread batter."

Grandma quickly rubbed the pans with a

little grease so that the bread wouldn't stick, and then helped hold the big bowl while Thurgood poured and spooned the batter into the pans. Grandma opened the oven door. Thurgood placed the pans into the hot oven and carefully closed the door.

"You watch the clock, Thurgood. The bread will be ready to come out in about twenty minutes."

Thurgood sat at the table, while his grandmother was washing up the dishes from their cooking. He thought about his grandfathers' names, and the names of his aunts and uncles. "Gram, where did you get the names for all your children?"

She hesitated a moment, and then dried her hands on her apron as she answered him. "Well, your grandpa chose most of the names. When he was at sea he sometimes would go to the theater when he was in port. He saw the opera *Norma* when he was in a port in Chile named Arica, so he named your mother Norma Arica. He saw some of Shakespeare's plays and he learned to enjoy Shakespeare. So he named Avonia Delicia and Avon after the river, Avon, which flows through Shakespeare's hometown, Stratford-upon-Avon."

"How did Aunt Denmedia get her name?"

"She was named for the grocery store, Denmedia Marketa."

"What about Uncle Fearless and Aunt Ravine?"

"Just because we liked the sound of their names, Fearless Mentor and Ravine Silestria," Grandma said. "Now that's enough. We need to set the table. Your grandfather will be coming in most any time and he'll be hungry. You set a place for yourself too. Your mama knows you will be staying for supper with us."

Thurgood looked at the clock. "It's almost time to take the corn bread out." The sweet odor of the baking corn bread filled the kitchen. It smelled so good, Thurgood could almost taste it!

Just then, the screen door slammed, and Grandpa, looking very grim, strode into the kitchen.

"What's wrong?" asked Grandma.

"Our next-door neighbor wants me to help repair the fence that runs between our houses. First time he's even bothered speaking to me!"

Thurgood thought about the crabby face of the white neighbor, as his grandfather went on.

"He said we're both Christians and that we both go to the same church. And we are going to end up in heaven together."

Grandma said, "Um . . . is that right!"

"Not me," growled Grandpa. "If he goes to heaven, I'm not!"

Furnace Room
Learning

The evening before Thurgood's first day at high school, his mother sat down at the kitchen table and told Thurgood to sit down opposite her. Her smooth face was serious as she said, "Thurgood, you have the opportunity to do very well in school. You are starting off with a fresh record, and it is up to you to make the most of your high school education. I expect you to do well!"

The first few days he was on his best

behavior. He dressed very carefully as he got ready for school. Aubrey and he walked to school together each morning. Their high school was in an old brick building, with dark, shabby classrooms. There was no gymnasium or auditorium, only a small play yard in the back. On their way to school, they walked past the big, new high school for the white kids, with its big gymnasium and spacious football field. It didn't seem right, but it was the way it was.

Uncle Cyrus Marshall was his algebra teacher, and Thurgood sat straight and tall at his desk in algebra class. He paid attention and listened carefully as Uncle Cyrus spoke. Each day Thurgood made sure that he finished all his homework and that it was correct. At the end of the semester, Thurgood had earned an A in his algebra class. He studied for his other classes, too, though not too hard, yet his grades were good.

Thurgood's parents were pleased when

Uncle Cyrus told them that Thurgood had the sharpest mind of any student he had ever taught. Aunt Elizabeth smiled as she heard her husband. She knew Thurgood was smart, but she thought Uncle Cyrus might be biased. Thurgood was his nephew. But he was not alone. Thurgood's other teachers thought Thurgood was a very bright student, too.

Thurgood enjoyed going to high school with his brother, Aubrey. He played football, joined a lot of the high school clubs, and had good times with his many friends. However, he also got into trouble with his friends. It wasn't too long before his mischief caught up with him, and he was sent to the principal, Mr. Lee!

Mr. Lee said nothing as he looked at the big, overgrown boy in front of him. Thurgood stood as he waited for the lecture he thought he would get. His hands and arms felt limp as they hung at his sides. He thought he might get a whipping. He knew sometimes kids could get whipped in the principal's office.

Mr. Lee put aside any thought of whipping the big, strong boy. He came up with a better form of punishment. He took a book from his desk and said, "Thurgood, you take this copy of the Constitution of the United States of America and go down to the furnace room in the basement. You are not to come up until you have memorized the Preamble."

Thurgood was surprised. He hadn't known what his punishment would be, but he thought this shouldn't be too bad. He took the copy of the Constitution and made his way down to the basement. He found an old wooden chair in the dark, dusty furnace room. He moved it over so that he could get light from the single, dim lightbulb. He sat down and started to read, and then to memorize. It wasn't easy as he repeated and repeated it to himself. Finally, when he thought he could remember so that he could

repeat it, he went back up to the principal's office. Mr. Lee listened patiently as Thurgood repeated the Preamble to the Constitution word for word.

"We, the people of the United States, in order to form a more perfect union, establish justice, insure domestic tranquillity, provide for the common defense, promote the general welfare, and secure the blessings of liberty to ourselves and our posterity, do ordain and establish this Constitution for the United States of America."

Mr. Lee nodded. "What does that mean?"

Thurgood frowned as he said the words to himself silently. Then he answered slowly, "I guess it means this is what the Constitution is going to do."

Mr. Lee nodded again and said, "That's right. The goal of the Constitution is to make sure all United States citizens will have justice and liberty." He hesitated and looked to see if Thurgood was paying attention, and then he said, "All right, you may go."

This was his first trip to the furnace room, but not the last! Every time Thurgood misbehaved in classes, or caused trouble at high school football games or dances, he was sent to the furnace room again.

Norma and Will Marshall were not happy that Thurgood got into so much trouble, but they thought the punishment was wise. At least he was learning the Constitution.

He pondered as he read and memorized parts of the Constitution, and he would bring his questions to his father at night. They had long conversations. "I don't understand what the Constitution does! Things aren't the same for black kids and white kids." He saw the lack of equality everywhere.

Will Marshall nodded, and Thurgood went on. "Our school for all our kids sure isn't equal to the white kids' school! Look at their big, new building . . . and football field . . . gym . . . and everything."

Will Marshall agreed as he shook his head and answered patiently, "The Constitution states how things *should* be, not the way they are."

One day after school, Thurgood went down into town on his way home, and he had a miserable experience, which he never forgot.

In Baltimore all the facilities were separate for white and colored—the drinking fountains, the toilets, and entrances to restaurants. Thurgood had gone downtown on the trolley car and soon he felt the need to go to the restroom. He looked and looked and could not find a toilet for colored people. He became more and more anxious when he couldn't find a toilet anywhere. He passed a public restroom for whites only in one of the stores, but he knew that he didn't dare go in, no matter how badly he needed to. He finally decided the only thing he could do was to get on a trolley and go home as quickly as he could. He was in pain by the time he reached his trolley stop. He hopped off the streetcar and ran to his front door. And when he reached the step, he just couldn't last any longer and he had an accident on his own front step! He was so embarrassed and so angry! He never forgot that moment of terrible embarrassment, which happened because he could not go into a restroom marked for whites only!

Thurgood Lands in Jail

Aubrey and Thurgood both had part-time jobs while they were in high school. Thurgood was glad to have a job as a delivery boy at Schoen's Dress Shop in Charles Street. Mr. Schoen made hats, and many of the richest, most important people in Baltimore were his customers. One day when he went to work, Mr. Schoen said, "Thurgood, I have several hats that need to be delivered right away."

As it started out there was nothing different about this day. But it turned out to be a day when Thurgood had reason to remember his father's words: "If anyone ever calls you "nigger," you not only have my permission to fight, you've got my orders to fight!"

Thurgood delivered hats for Mr. Schoen every day. He liked his job. The people to whom the hats were delivered were always pleased to get them, and it was always fun for Thurgood to see different parts of the city. He asked, "Where do I go, Mr. Schoen?"

The shop owner leaned over his records, and tore off the sales slip with the address and handed it to Thurgood. "You'll need to take the trolley. The address is right here on this slip." He told Thurgood to put his arms out, and he stacked the hatboxes one on top of the other.

Thurgood clutched the boxes tightly so he wouldn't drop any of them.

"Is that all right? Can you carry all of

those?" Mr. Schoen asked as he helped by adjusting the boxes so they were squarely on top of each other.

Thurgood felt so important. "Of course, this is fine," he said confidently, and he balanced the boxes carefully as he went out the door.

He walked down the street to the trolley stop. His stack of boxes was so high he had trouble seeing over them. At the trolley stop he saw Mr. Truesdale, one of his father's friends, and they talked while they were waiting for the trolley. When he heard the trolley screech to a stop, he stepped forward to climb on.

Then, suddenly, someone grabbed his arm and pulled him off the step! The hatboxes flew everywhere! A small white man shouted, "Nigger! Don't you *ever* step in front of a white woman again!"

Thurgood was furious! This man had made him drop all of Mr. Schoen's hats, and he had

called him a bad word! He swung around and without a second thought punched the man in the stomach. The white man hit back. Thurgood could feel the blood rush to his face, and the thud of his heartbeats in his throat. He was so angry! He swung his fists, hitting and jabbing furiously. Mr. Truesdale said, "Thurgood, stop. Don't fight!" And then he appealed to the white man. "Don't . . . please don't. He's just a boy!" But neither of them paid any attention to his pleas as they continued punching each other!

A crowd gathered around to watch the fight, and the two were still fighting when a policeman pulled them apart! Thurgood was still swinging his arms, even though the policeman was holding him away from the other man. When the policeman grabbed him, Thurgood knew he was in trouble, but he was so angry that he didn't even care. He was breathing so hard that he had a hard time calming down. When he saw that the policeman was Army Matthews, he felt a little better. He knew that Officer Matthews would be fair.

The crowd lingered to see what was going to happen, and several people were trying to tell what had happened. One man said, "That boy hit the white man for no reason at all!"

Mr. Truesdale was quiet. He didn't want to get in trouble, but finally he had to say, "That man called Thurgood a bad name and pulled him off the trolley."

"That boy pushed in front of a white lady," a white bystander shouted.

Police Officer Army Matthews turned to Thurgood and asked quietly, "Thurgood, tell me what happened."

"I was just getting on the trolley with all my hatboxes, when that man grabbed me, called me a nigger, and pulled me off the trolley steps—and he made me drop all my hatboxes!" Thurgood said breathlessly.

Officer Matthews listened to Thurgood.

Then he turned to the white man, and heard his side of the story. He didn't know which of them to believe, and so he took them both to the police station.

Thurgood resisted, "I've got to pick up the hats!"

"All right," said Officer Matthews, and he helped as they tried to pick up the hatboxes scattered all over the sidewalk.

Thurgood got a sudden empty feeling in the pit of his stomach. For the first time he realized how much trouble he was in. He was lucky that Officer Matthews was the policeman. Many other police officers would not have even listened to him. They would just have blamed him, no matter what had actually happened!

Thurgood sat on the bench in the police station as Officer Matthews wrote up the arrest. He rubbed his sweaty face with his hands and shook his head. He was being arrested! He thought about Al and some of the boys in the alley and how often some of them were arrested—and even sent to jail!

He dropped his head in his hands. He knew that he was in big trouble for hitting a white man. He probably would lose his job. Then he shivered as he felt cold chills up and down his arms. What if he were put in jail! He would be kicked out of school. What would his parents say! He took a deep breath. He knew his father would agree that he had the right to defend himself! But that didn't make him feel much better, because he knew his parents would be so disappointed if he had to go to jail.

He couldn't believe it when Officer Matthews came to him and said, "Thurgood, you are free to go now. Mr. Schoen paid your fine."

Thurgood looked up and saw the white store owner, and his first thought was he wondered how Mr. Schoen knew about what had happened. Mr. Schoen was putting the receipt for the fine in his well-worn leather wallet. It was hard to know what he was thinking. His ruddy, broad face with his shining eyeglasses had no expression.

"Mr. Schoen, I'm sorry about the hats." Thurgood didn't know what to say. "I tried to pick them up."

"You don't need to say anything, Thurgood." Mr. Schoen answered in a kind voice. "I understand." Then he went on almost as if he were talking to himself. "Maybe better than you know."

Together they gathered up the stack of battered hatboxes and carried them along as they walked down the steps from the police station. Thurgood took a deep breath. It felt good to be outside and away from that stuffy, frightening police station.

"You're going home now?" asked Mr. Schoen.

"Don't you want me to take the hats back to the shop? I guess it's too late to deliver them now," Thurgood said slowly.

"I can get them. You just go on home now."

"Okay." Thurgood nodded and turned to walk down the street.

"Then I'll see you at work after school tomorrow."

"You mean I still have my job? You're not going—" Thurgood was going to say "you're not going to fire me," but Mr. Schoen interrupted him, saying, "Of course, you still have your job. Just be on time!"

Thurgood ran all the way home, and bounded up the steps and in the door. The moment his mother saw him she knew something was wrong. His hair was tousled, his face was sweaty and dirty, and his shirt was torn. Aubrey was sitting at the kitchen table doing his homework. When he saw Thurgood he exclaimed, "You've been in a fight! Where is the other guy?"

Thurgood told them what had happened, how he had been trying to get on the trolley and hadn't been able to see over his hatboxes. A white man had accused him of pushing in front of a white lady, and had called him "nigger."

"And what did you do?" Aubrey demanded.

"I hit him!"

Mother's face tightened, and her jaw was firm, "You hit him!" She was shocked! "You mean you hit him first?"

Thurgood nodded as he pressed his lips together.

"That was pretty dumb!" shouted Aubrey. "You were so stupid to hit a white man!"

Thurgood didn't reply. He knew what an awful chance he had taken. A Negro boy was not supposed to push in front of white folks, and certainly was not supposed to hit a white man. He was thoughtful as he remembered what his father had told him. He still felt he was right to defend himself when that man had grabbed him and called him a bad name!

But he knew he was lucky that Army

Matthews had been the police officer and that Mr. Schoen was his friend. He knew he needed to be wiser from now on, and he didn't want to upset his mother.

The Constitution and Its Amendments

Thurgood and his brother were very different. Aubrey was quiet and studious, while Thurgood was full of fun and enjoyed having a good time. Thurgood made good grades in high school, but Aubrey's grades were always better.

Thurgood missed his brother when Aubrey graduated from high school and went to

Lincoln University. He looked forward to the weekends and holidays when Aubrey would come home and tell him all about college and the things he was doing.

He thought when Aubrey went away to college, he wouldn't have to be compared to him anymore. But he was wrong. Even though Aubrey was not at Frederick Douglass High School with him, Thurgood still had to live up to Aubrey's reputation as the smart, top student.

At the beginning of the school year, Thurgood walked into his first class of the day. The teacher was sitting behind the desk. The teacher, a short, dark man, was leaning over his classbook on the desk. He looked up at Thurgood and asked in a grumpy voice, "Your name?"

Thurgood answered politely, "Thurgood Marshall."

"Marshall . . . Marshall," he repeated as he looked for the name on his class list. And then he looked over the top of his glasses at Thurgood and asked, "Is Aubrey Marshall your brother?"

"Yes, sir," Thurgood replied as he thought to himself, *Here it comes*—and it did.

The teacher's expression did not change as he said, "I hope you are as smart as your brother. I'll expect very good work from you." But as he said it, he looked at Thurgood as if he didn't really think he would be as smart as Aubrey. Thurgood just groaned to himself.

The teacher frowned as he stared at Thurgood, and said sharply, "What did you say!"

Thurgood hadn't meant to groan out loud. "Nothing, sir," he said hastily, and went to the back of the room to take his seat.

Studying just was not the most important thing in Thurgood's life. He had many friends and lots of good times. He loved to go to the dances. He had many dates with pretty girls. He played football and was always ready to have fun. Sometimes he had too much fun.

One time he and several of his friends planned a prank that they were going to play on one of the assistant principals. The prank did not work out as they had thought it would. They planned to embarrass the young assistant principal, but the plan backfired and instead the joke was on them! And they were all punished.

As usual, Thurgood was sent to the furnace room again, and this time Mr. Lee said loudly in total exasperation, "I do not want to see you again until you have memorized all of the amendments to the Constitution!"

Thurgood took the book containing the Constitution and its amendments under his arm and made his way down the basement stairs. Then he heard Mr. Lee come to the top of the stairs to shout, "I want you to study and be able to tell me about the Thirteenth, Fourteenth, and Fifteenth Amendments!"

Thurgood had already memorized the first

ten amendments—the Bill of Rights. He worked on memorizing the Eleventh Amendment and the long, long Twelfth Amendment about the election of the president of the United States. The dark basement room grew even darker as dusk was falling at the end of the day. There was only one small dusty window, and it was almost as dark outside as it was inside in the basement. He pulled the string to turn on the dim light bulb, and wondered how much longer he would have to stay.

Soon he heard Mr. Lee's voice. As much as he didn't want to see the principal, he was glad to hear him say, "Thurgood, you may come up now. You take the Constitution book home with you tonight, and tomorrow you can go straight down to the basement until you have completed all nineteen amendments."

Thurgood hurried up the stairs, got his coat and books, and walked home slowly. The bare tree branches threaded their black limbs across the dark gray sky. He felt as grim as the dark day. He didn't know how he would explain to his mother and dad that he was in trouble again. He really was sorry. He hadn't meant to get into trouble. It just had seemed like it would be fun to embarrass the assistant principal, who was just so right all the time! He guessed if he thought more about what he did, he wouldn't get in so much trouble.

He let himself in the front door and went into the dark house. His mother was not home from school yet, and his father was at work at the Gibson Island Club. He felt lonely in the empty house, but in a way he was glad that he didn't have to explain what had happened. He sighed. He knew that Mr. Lee had probably called his mother.

He went upstairs and stretched out across his bed. He was so tall that his feet hung over the edge of the bed. He turned on the overhead light and got out the Constitution.

He might as well work on learning the amendments and get it over with.

He rolled over on his stomach, put the book in front of him, and read the Thirteenth Amendment. It didn't take him long to memorize this amendment, which abolished slavery. He frowned as he thought about it. He couldn't imagine how it would be to be a slave, to be owned by a master who had complete control of your life. And then he thought about the master, and he couldn't imagine what it would be like to be a slave owner, to be the owner of another person.

Thurgood read and reread the first section of the Fourteenth Amendment, which guarantees equal rights to all people. And then he went on to read the Fifteenth Amendment, which gives the right to vote to everyone regardless of "race, color, or previous condition of servitude."

Suddenly he heard the front door open and his mother's steps clicking sharply on the floor as she went straight through the house to the bottom of the stairs. "Thurgood," she called, "you can just stay up there in your room until your dad comes home."

It seemed to Thurgood the evening stretched on forever. He lay on the bed and read and reread and memorized until he was tired. Then he got up and sat in the straight chair at his desk and memorized some more. And then he paced back and forth, and repeated the words aloud. It wasn't hard to remember Section 1 of the Fourteenth Amendment, which guaranteed the rights of citizenship and equal rights to all, nor the Fifteenth Amendment, which guaranteed the right of all citizens to vote. But he spent a lot of time trying to remember all the other parts of the amendments.

Finally he heard his father open the door and come in the house, and then his mother's and father's voices as they talked. He took a deep breath. He knew he was in for it, but he was anxious to get it over with, and he wanted to talk to his father about the Constitution.

Will Marshall's voice was stern as he called Thurgood to come downstairs. Thurgood sat down at the kitchen table as his father stood. His father was very serious as he lectured Thurgood on the importance of his education, and that getting into mischief was a terrible waste of his time, and the time of the teachers and principals who were trying to teach him.

Thurgood's father's voice had gotten louder as he was scolding his son. Then he sat down, and said in a quieter tone, "At least you are learning the Constitution." His thin face was drawn from the exertion of being angry with Thurgood, and weary from the fatigue of the hard work of serving the members and guests of the Gibson Island Club.

"I'm memorizing the amendments to the Constitution, and I don't understand the Fourteenth and Fifteenth," Thurgood blurted.

His father thought he knew what Thurgood was asking, but he said, "What don't you understand?"

"Don't they give equal rights to all the people in the United States?"

"That is the intent—"

"But why is it that white people have more rights than Negroes?" Thurgood interrupted.

Will Marshall continued, "These three important amendments, the Thirteenth, Fourteenth, and Fifteenth, were passed quickly after the Civil War. They set out the way things *should* be. But then twenty-five or thirty years later the United States Supreme Court made a decision that states could have 'separate but equal' facilities for whites and Negroes."

Thurgood said, "Our schools are separate all right, but they sure aren't equal!"

Thurgood and his father sat at the table and talked for a very long time about the Constitution and its amendments.

❉   ❉   ❉

By the time Thurgood had finished high school he knew all the Constitution and its amendments by heart! He was sixteen years old when he graduated from Frederick Douglass High School in 1925, and he and his parents had decided that he too would go to Lincoln University. He felt he was ready to go away to school. He was confident in his ability to get the education that he knew was so important to him. Though his mother wanted him to become a dentist, he didn't really know yet what he wanted to be, but he knew that he could be successful no matter what career he chose.

College was expensive. The Marshalls were so eager for their sons to get good educations, that they paid as much as they could toward their college bills. Aubrey and Thurgood both got summer jobs to earn as much money as they could to help, too.

Thurgood's father got him a job with the

B & O Railroad on the New York to Washington run. That first summer before he started at Lincoln University, he worked as a waiter in the dining car. When he started to work, the chief steward brought out a uniform. Thurgood held the pants up. They looked too short.

"Put them on," said the chief steward.

"I don't think they'll fit," Thurgood said.

"Put them on! You can't know until you try them!" the chief steward said impatiently.

Reluctantly, Thurgood pulled the pants on. He looked down and had to laugh, he looked like he was going wading. The pants were about four inches too short!

"Put the jacket on," instructed the chief steward.

Thurgood did as he was told, but he looked down at those high-water pants and said, "These are too short. I need a pair of longer pants." He felt so awkward in those short pants.

The chief steward looked at the boy with the high-water pants and said, "I can get another boy to fit into those pants, easier than I can get another pair of pants to fit you. If you want the job, just scooch down in them a little more."

And Thurgood scooched!

College Life

Thurgood spent the summer after his high school graduation working in the dining cars of the B & O Railroad in his ill-fitting steward's uniform. Although Thurgood was still fascinated with the trains clickety-clacking through the countryside, working in the dining car did not have the glamour that he had felt when he had visited the trains in the station with his father. He had to hurry to keep up serving so many diners in the dining car. The aisle was narrow and it was hard to serve large platters of food and pour coffee from hot coffee pots. There was very little time for him to look out the windows at the countryside.

As he worked he thought about going to Lincoln University at the end of summer, and with each train trip, he knew he was that much closer to being there.

Thurgood was excited when September finally came and he set off with Aubrey for Lincoln University. He didn't feel like a brand-new freshman when he arrived, because he had heard Aubrey talk about Lincoln for the past three years.

Lincoln University, outside Philadelphia, Pennsylvania, had been founded in 1854, before the Civil War, for men of color. The man who founded Lincoln University had come from Princeton University, and many of the faculty were from Princeton, too. Lincoln University was one of the very best colleges for Negro men, and the students at Lincoln called it the "black Princeton." At

146

the time Thurgood went to Lincoln, there were only about three hundred students. The professors were all white, and the students were all black males. No girls were admitted at this time.

When Aubrey and Thurgood arrived at the campus, Aubrey asked, "Do you want me to take you to your freshman dormitory where you will be living?" Because Aubrey was going to be a senior, he would live in a different section of the dorms.

Thurgood didn't answer right away. He couldn't believe that he was finally in college, and that he was here at Lincoln at last. He just stood and looked at the old red brick buildings among the majestic tall trees. Pathways to the buildings wound through the lawns of green. Slowly he answered, "Just tell me which building, and I'll go on my own to my dorm."

Aubrey pointed, and said, "It's that first

building on your right; just go on in and there will be someone at the desk to tell you how to get to your room. I'll go on to my dormitory, and I'll see you later."

Thurgood nodded, and carrying his suitcases, he walked on slowly through the beautiful campus. He looked around him as he walked. He saw other students also carrying their belongings, headed for the freshman dorm.

It didn't take Thurgood long to settle in, and he made many friends. There were many interesting students who were attending Lincoln University. One of his good friends was Cab Calloway, who later became a famous bandleader. Many of the students' parents were teachers and preachers, but also many of the students came from working-class families. There were also students from Africa at Lincoln. Two of these African students went on to become leaders in their own countries. Kwame Nkrumah later became the first prime minister and president of Ghana, and Benjamin Nnamdi Azikiwe became the first president of Nigeria.

Thurgood had a wonderful time at Lincoln University. His parents had sent him there to get a good education, and he did despite the fact that he didn't study much and spent a lot of his spare time having fun. He loved to play cards, go to parties, sing and dance, take the train into nearby Philadelphia, and hang out with his many friends.

Most of the students had part-time jobs, and one of Thurgood's jobs was to work in the school bakery. Several of his friends also worked in the bakery, and they had a good time there, too. It was so hot they all worked with their shirts off as they mixed the dough and kneaded the bread. After the night's work was finished, Thurgood would take a loaf of hot, freshly baked bread, cut the top, and fill the loaf with a pound of butter. And it was so good!

The professors all lived in their homes off campus, and they didn't pay a lot of attention to what the students did in their free time. And so, outside of their classrooms, the students behaved in any way they wanted to. The upperclassmen were really hard on the freshmen. They went out of their way to make the freshmen feel like the lowest students in school. They made them do silly things, and they sometimes paddled them with wooden paddles.

At Christmastime of 1925, twenty-three-year-old Langston Hughes, a well-known poet, entered Lincoln University as a student. All of the students were talking about Hughes, whose book of poetry, *The Weary Blues*, had just been published. Thurgood got a copy of Langston Hughes's book. He loved to read the poems, which were written in what Thurgood called, "country talk."

Langston Hughes's dorm room was just

down the hall from Thurgood's and they became good friends. The upperclassmen really worked at making life difficult for Hughes, because he was older than the other freshmen. And they wanted to make themselves feel more important by hazing a well-known author.

Then the following year, when Thurgood and his friends were sophomores, they took their turn in harassing the incoming freshman class. They enjoyed graduating from the lowly status of freshmen, and got a great deal of pleasure in making life difficult for the new freshmen. They made the freshmen call them "Sir" and, in any way they could, they made life difficult for the new students.

Thurgood and his sophomore friends got together and thought of all the unpleasant things they could do. They finally came up with the very worst indignity of all: They decided to shave the heads of the freshmen!

It took a lot of planning, but one night twenty-six of the sophomores, including Thurgood, shaved the heads of almost all the freshmen!

The professors were outraged, and the administration threatened to expel Thurgood and all the sophomores who had been involved. This group of sopho-more students got together and worried about how they could get out of this mess they had gotten themselves into. None of them had planned that they would cause this much trouble. Thurgood felt terri-ble. He couldn't even imagine what his parents would do if he were expelled from school!

The sophomore students appointed Langston Hughes to write an apology, to admit that they had been wrong in doing what they had done, and to ask that they be allowed to stay in school.

The administration withdrew the discipline, and the sophomore culprits were permitted to

remain in school. After nearly being expelled from school, Thurgood decided that he had better take his education more seriously.

For a while he studied more, and his grades improved, but soon he recovered from his fright of almost being kicked out of school, and though he studied enough to make passing grades, he spent most of his time having fun. He loved having debates with his friends in the dormitory. He usually won the debates because he had so much practice arguing with his father and Aubrey in their dinner table discussions. He joined the school debating club. He read many books as he gathered material for his arguments in debating. He gained the name "Wrathful Marshall" because he always won.

Thurgood took great pleasure in his ability to influence other people with his debating. The football team at Lincoln University was a consistent loser, and they had not won a game all season. Thurgood decided to give a speech at a pep rally—and the team tied their next game. Was this just a coincidence? Thurgood was sure his pep rally speech had done it!

Equal Rights at
the Movie Theater

Crystal white snow lay heavily on the tree
branches, and the water on the pond was
frozen to an icy glaze. Some of the students
were gliding merrily as they skated around
the pond, but Thurgood and Cab Calloway
were having a snowball fight with some of the
guys from their dormitory. The fight ended
with Thurgood and Cab running after their
friends, who had ducked into the dorm to get
away from them.

Thurgood and Cab peeled off their warm winter coats and hats, and ran to the kitchen where they got pans and long-handled wooden spoons. They started beating out rhythms on the pans and running up and down the halls. They sang and played with gusto. Finally, John Little opened his room door and said, "Marshall and Calloway, you are the noisiest guys in the dorm! Come on in and be quiet!"

Laughing, Thurgood and Cab Calloway tumbled into the room where a group of the guys were sitting on the floor, and lounging on the beds as they were talking.

Bob was saying, "Why don't we go to the movies next week? There's going to be a good western movie playing."

"You mean at the theater in Oxford?" asked Len. "There's always a cowboy and Indian movie playing!"

The nearest movie theater was in the small nearby town of Oxford. When the students from Lincoln University went to that theater, they were never allowed to sit in the seats on the main floor. After they bought their tickets for the movie, they were told to go up to the balcony. Thurgood and his friends thought this was really stupid, but they had always followed the rules of the movie theater without argument.

"Why should we go to see their dumb western movies?" William asked. "They act like they're doing us a favor by letting us sit in their balcony!"

"Why don't we do something about it!" John Little demanded. "It is really ridiculous that we are hustled off to the balcony to sit! We pay admission like all the other people. Why shouldn't we sit where we want to!"

"Well, maybe," Bob answered timidly, "but I'd rather sit in the balcony."

"Dandy! If that's where you want to sit, but it should be your choice, not someone telling you where you have to sit!" retorted Little.

"Okay, next time we go to the movies, let's sit downstairs," Thurgood said.

"The theater people aren't going to let us," said Bob.

"So?" said John Little. "We need to get organized. Let's get a group together and go this Friday night. If enough of us go, and we all go in at the same time—"

One of the others said, "You're kidding. They're going to shove us upstairs to the balcony just like they always do."

"But we don't have to do it!" Little shouted back. "We can just walk right in to the seats on the main floor."

"They won't let us do that."

"How can they stop us?" Little asked. "We need to have at least ten or fifteen of us go in at the same time. How can that one scrawny little usher stop us?"

"He could call the police!" Bob answered fearfully.

Little laughed. "Have you seen the police in Oxford?"

"What do you mean?"

"The police force in Oxford is one very overweight officer! It would take a long time for him to even get there, and if we had to, we could outrun him!"

Bob decided that he didn't want to go. He didn't want to cause any trouble. "Okay, that's fine." John turned to Thurgood and said, "Talk to your friends and find as many as you can to go with us. The more the better!"

Little and Thurgood passed the word around. "We're going to go to the movie theater on Friday night and sit on the main floor! What about coming along?"

There was an undercurrent of excitement all week. All of the planning and talk was done quietly. On Friday night, John Little, Thurgood, Cranston, and three of their friends climbed into Cranston's roadster and roared down the road to Oxford to the movie. Confidently they walked up to the ticket window and bought their tickets just like they always had in the past. Thurgood smiled to himself as he watched the ticket seller push the tickets toward John. He felt a secret delight that they knew something that she didn't know. This evening was going to be different. The young lady did not even look up as she said just as she had always done in the past, "You'll have to sit in the balcony."

As Thurgood walked into the theater he saw two more groups of Lincoln students coming up behind them. It felt good to see they had such a large group. They walked past the stairs to stride right down the aisle to seats at the front and center on the main floor. Fortunately the theater was not very crowded and there were plenty of seats. The young usher tried to stop them saying, "You can't sit here; you need to sit up in the balcony." They didn't pay any attention to him and pushed past him to the vacant seats. As they were taking their seats the other groups of Lincoln students followed them in and filed into the vacant seats two or three rows behind them.

COLORED
SEATING

A white man watched as they took their seats. He saw how they had pushed right past the usher, who had just stood there for a few minutes doing nothing. Finally the usher said again, "You'll have to go on up to the seats in the balcony. You can't sit here."

When the students did not pay any attention to him, the young usher stood as though he didn't know what to do next. And then he just walked up the aisle to the back of the theater.

The white man stood up when he saw the usher wasn't going to do anything about the black students sitting on the first floor. His face reddened with anger as he moved from his seat to an empty seat behind Thurgood. He leaned forward to whisper, "Why don't you move out of here and go up in the balcony where you belong!"

Thurgood replied in a calm voice, "I paid for my ticket, and I can sit wherever I want to."

"You can sit wherever the theater management says you can, and that's in the balcony!"

growled the man in a husky whisper.

"I choose to sit right here," Thurgood replied.

The man continued to whisper his angry remarks, and Thurgood simply looked forward at the screen and ignored him. Thurgood thought how strange it was. He didn't even feel like the man had a face, it was just as though his face was just an ugly feeling. Finally the man moved away back to his own seat.

After the movie was over, the boys wondered what might happen, but they walked out with all the other theatergoers and no one said anything to them. It was just as though they were invisible.

Thurgood said afterward that it didn't feel so good being invisible, but at least it was better than being insulted and shown disrespect.

After that Lincoln students sat wherever they wanted to when they went to the movies at the Oxford movie theater.

Law School
and a Career

In Thurgood Marshall's third year at Lincoln University he met a beautiful young girl with whom he fell in love. Several of the Lincoln University students, including Thurgood, attended the Cherry Street Memorial Church in Philadelphia, where they looked forward to meeting young ladies. And it was there that he met Vivian Burey, a student at the University of Pennsylvania. He and Vivian, whom he called Buster, decided to marry the summer after their junior year in college.

Their parents, both the Marshalls and the Bureys, thought they were too young, but the young couple persuaded their parents that they were ready for marriage, and the wedding took place the summer before Thurgood's senior year at Lincoln. After their marriage Buster did not return to school and took a job as a secretary in Oxford.

For the first time, Thurgood became really serious about his education. He and Buster took an apartment in Oxford. He worked at his part-time job, went to his classes, studied long hours, and spent his free time with Buster. He didn't have time to play cards, or sit around and talk with his friends in the dorm.

As his senior year went on, more and more Thurgood doubted that he wanted to be a dentist. And as he spent time studying, reading in the library, and debating in the Lincoln

Debate Society, he decided that he wanted to be a lawyer. Though his mother was sorry that he was not going into dentistry, his father was pleased. He was convinced that Thurgood would make a fine lawyer.

Thurgood graduated from Lincoln University in 1930 with honors, which meant that he had earned excellent grades in his studies, and most especially in his senior year after his marriage to Buster.

The June day was warm, as the graduates lined up to march down the aisle to the speaker's platform where they would receive their diplomas. Will and Norma Marshall sat in the front row with Thurgood's wife, Buster. When Thurgood's name was announced and presented his diploma with honors, Will and Norma looked at each other with pride. Norma smiled, and her eyes filled with tears. It made her so happy to have two fine sons who had graduated from college. And Aubrey was very close to finishing his medical education and would soon be a fully qualified doctor. She knew now Thurgood wasn't going to be a dentist, but she was satisfied that he would be a lawyer.

That summer, Buster and he both had jobs, but it was hard to save money to go on to school. Thurgood shook his head. "I don't see how we can afford for me to go to law school. It's so hard to get a job. Maybe we should just keep the jobs we have. Maybe sometime later we can get enough money for law school."

Buster set her mouth. "Of course you are going to law school. This is very important. I'm sure we can manage, with what I make and with what you can make working part-time."

This was a time when many people did not have jobs and money was very scarce. Thurgood thought perhaps he should work and try to help with the family expenses, but

Buster and his parents all agreed that he should go to law school.

"If I can go to the University of Maryland Law School right here in Baltimore, tuition to the state school is not too expensive. I could ride the trolley to classes, which wouldn't cost much and would only be a ten-minute ride. That would mean I could have more time to work at a part-time job." Thurgood thought that maybe this way he could afford to go to law school.

Thurgood applied to the all-white University of Maryland Law School. In short order, he received a very brief, curt letter that said that he would not be admitted to the University of Maryland Law School. He was refused admission because he was a black student. He was disappointed at being turned down, but more than that he was angry!

He then applied to, and was accepted, at the Howard University Law School in

Washington, D.C., which was the black law school nearest to Baltimore. Howard University, which was founded in 1867, was the largest black university in the United States.

Norma and Will Marshall told Thurgood and Buster that they could live with them so that Thurgood could afford to go to law school. They also said they would try to help with some of the money he needed for tuition.

As Thurgood and Buster counted up the money for school expenses, they saw it wasn't enough. Again Thurgood thought maybe he wouldn't be able to go to law school. Norma Marshall said without a moment of doubt, "You are going!" She didn't hesitate as she looked at her engagement and wedding rings. She knew what she could do.

Norma Marshall walked down the street to the pawnshop, took off her rings, and gathered up the money that the pawnshop man gave her. He said, "You know you can get your rings back when you pay back the money."

She nodded and walked out of the shop without looking back.

Thurgood and Buster moved into Thurgood's old room in his parents' home. Buster got a job as a secretary in Baltimore. Thurgood found a part-time job and started attending Howard University Law School.

The year Thurgood Marshall started law school, Howard University Law School had a new dean. Charles Hamilton Houston set about making Howard University Law School a much better, more respected law school. He brought new well-qualified black law professors to teach fewer law students in a more demanding program.

Though Thurgood really enjoyed his courses at law school, he had a very difficult schedule. He had to get up at 5:30 in the morning to take a train to Washington in time for school. Then he had to take the train at 3:00 in the afternoon to get back for his job in Baltimore. After work he had his evening meal and then studied until after midnight every night.

At the end of his first year, he had earned the best grades of all the students in his class. Because he was the top student he was offered a job in the Howard University Law School Library. This made it much easier for him to work and go to school at Howard.

Charles Hamilton Houston taught some classes as well as being dean, and he was a very demanding instructor. Charles Houston himself had earned his law degree at Harvard University and had been an honor student. He had practiced law in Washington for a time, but he was glad to have the opportunity to be a professor and dean at Howard University. He felt that there was a need for bright, well-educated black lawyers to work for the rights that the Constitution promised.

He welcomed the opportunity to be able to train young black law students.

Houston expected a great deal from his students. He told them that they needed not only to be good, but to be the very best. He had a class in civil rights, where his students could learn about the rights of personal liberty. They studied the Constitution and especially the amendments that promised equal rights to all. Thurgood was one of Houston's best students. He already knew the Constitution and its amendments by heart.

It was clear to these young black law students that not all Americans had equal treatment under the law. Most of these young men had been refused admission to law schools only because they were black. Thurgood thought about how he had been refused admission to the University of Maryland Law School.

From Charles Houston they gained the understanding that it could be shown the

Constitution was not being followed. At first Thurgood thought Charles Houston was a very tough professor whose classes were difficult. But he soon discovered that Houston was always fair, and that his goal was to teach his students so that they would become the best lawyers they could be. He brought to his students an enthusiasm that they could make a difference with the legal battle for equality for all American citizens. Thurgood had great admiration for Charles Houston and wanted to follow in his footsteps.

Thurgood Marshall also learned a great deal from Law Professor William Henry Hastie. The professors at Howard not only taught their students, they also took on outside cases to help black people. Then they had their students help them in the preparation for taking these cases to court. Thurgood learned from Professor Hastie how to prepare written arguments for actual cases.

Thurgood worked on the case of a young

black student who had been turned down by the University of North Carolina School of Pharmacy. Thurgood went to the library and gathered all the information that would be important to the case. He reread the Thirteenth and Fourteenth Amendments to the Constitution, which he remembered so well. Then he read the information on the Supreme Court decision that had set up the opportunity for the states to have "separate but equal" schools for black students.

Professor Hastie and Thurgood, with some of the other students, checked the money spent by the State of North Carolina on black and white schools. It was clear that much more money was spent on the white schools than on the black schools.

From all of this evidence Thurgood wrote the brief, which is the written argument for the case. Professor Hastie was very impressed with the fine, logical brief that Thurgood had written.

All of the law students were sure that Professor Hastie would win the case, proving that the State of North Carolina did not have a separate and equal pharmacy school for black students, and that the student, Thomas Hocutt, should be admitted to the state university.

Thurgood Marshall and the other students were shocked when the case was lost. They could not understand the unfairness of the verdict. Charles Houston and William Hastie were disappointed, but they knew this was one small step toward their goal of gaining equal rights for everyone. And they would appeal the decision.

Marshall graduated from Howard University Law School in 1933 at the top of his class. After graduation Thurgood Marshall set up a law office in Baltimore, but times were hard and it was very difficult to make a living. The clients who came to Marshall had little or no money, but he tried to help them anyway.

Charles Houston joined the National Association for the Advancement of Colored People in New York City as their chief counsel, and he persuaded the Baltimore branch to hire Thurgood.

Soon Thurgood Marshall learned that a young black man, Donald Murray, a graduate of Amherst College, who had applied for admission to the law school of the University of Maryland, had been turned down. Marshall was eager to take on the challenge of the fight with the university. He still felt hurt that the University of Maryland had refused to admit him to their law school. He filed the documents asking the Baltimore city court to require the university to admit Murray to the law school in the fall semester.

Charles Houston came to Maryland to help Thurgood Marshall when this very important case went to trial on June 18, 1935.

After hearing that the university had admitted citizens of any other racial group, but never a Negro citizen, Judge O'Dunne made up his mind quickly, and handed down his decision that Donald Murray should be admitted to the law school of the University of Maryland.

Houston, Marshall, and Murray were all delighted, but Thurgood was especially pleased with their victory over the University of Maryland!

"Mr. Civil Rights"

In 1936, Charles Houston offered Thurgood Marshall a job with the National Association for the Advancement of Colored People in New York, and Buster and Thurgood moved to New York City. In 1938 Charles Houston returned to the private practice of law and Thurgood became the chief legal counsel for the NAACP. Then, later, Marshall was named the director and chief counsel for the Legal Defense and Educational Fund.

Thurgood Marshall went all over the United States, defending the rights of the people, and arguing their cases in court. He argued the voting rights of Negroes, the right to serve on a jury, and the right to a fair trial in cases when a person was accused of a crime. He felt strongly that equal rights were guaranteed under the law, and that the problems could and should be solved within the law.

As he traveled he stayed in the homes of friends, because there were no hotels for blacks. Often there were no restaurants where he could eat. He was threatened and sometimes had to leave towns in a chase in order to escape injury.

Thurgood helped organize teachers in Maryland to join the NAACP in a campaign to sue for equal pay. Thurgood's own mother had worked many years as a teacher in the Baltimore schools, but she had always been paid less than the white teachers with the same teaching positions. After several years the NAACP was successful, and finally for the first time Norma Marshall earned the same pay as the white teachers!

Norma Marshall was so proud of her son Thurgood, who was achieving a real difference in making life equal for all people. She was so proud of both her sons, Thurgood, the lawyer, and Aubrey, the doctor.

Thurgood was completely dedicated to his goal of working for equal rights for all people. Along with his serious work, though, he always had a fine sense of humor and enjoyed good stories and good times with his friends. He never got over his love of trains, and he had an electric train set up in his own home. He would put on his engineer's cap and set the electric trains to fly around the tracks as his hobby. He also never forgot his grandmother Mary Eliza's cooking lessons, and he enjoyed cooking his famous she-crab soup, corn bread, and other specialties for his family and friends.

Thurgood Marshall spent years with the

NAACP defending the rights of black people in a court of law. He was constant in pursuing his goal, which Charles Houston had stated, "to do away with all forms of segregation" in American law.

In 1952 he argued the case of Brown versus the Board of Education of Topeka, Kansas, before the U.S. Supreme Court. There were five different cases where black students had been denied equal opportunities of education. Finally, after long years in the lower courts, the case went to the U.S. Supreme Court. These five cases were joined together and were known by the name of the first of the cases, Brown versus Board of Education of Topeka. Though the Fourteenth Amendment of the Constitution of the United States guaranteed equal protection of the law to all citizens, in 1896 the Supreme Court had ruled that a state could maintain "separate but equal" facilities for blacks and whites. Separate schools were acceptable so long as the facilities were equal for black and white students.

Thurgood Marshall and the Legal Defense Fund staff worked very hard to prepare their case to show that these separate schools did not provide equal education. They knew how very important their presentation was to the Supreme Court! Eighty-one-year-old John W. Davis, one of the most well-known, respected lawyers in the country, was representing their opposition, and had argued many cases successfully before the Supreme Court.

Standing before the nine justices of the highest court of the land, in his clear rich voice, Thurgood Marshall argued the case that the facilities in separate schools were not equal for black and white students. He listed the evidence that these schools were in fact separate and unequal! His arguments were clear and well documented. He quoted numbers showing that southern states spent half as much for the schools for black students as they spent on schools for white students. He called psychologists and teachers as witnesses who testified that segregated schools contributed to poor self-esteem for black children. His conclusion was clear. This separate school system did not provide equal education for African-Americans.

A year later there had been no answer to the case. The Supreme Court called for more information and answers to a list of questions. Again Thurgood Marshall and John Davis argued their cases before the Supreme Court in December of 1953.

The Court was silent on the case for almost another six months. And then on May 17, 1954, Chief Justice Earl Warren read the unanimous decision of the court. "We conclude that in the field of public education the doctrine of 'separate but equal' has no place.

Separate educational facilities are inherently unequal."

This was the first great victory! But the fight had just begun, and Thurgood Marshall stood in the forefront of the continuing battles in courtroom after courtroom to maintain and gain equality for all people.

Marshall was grieved that Charles Houston, his longtime friend and mentor died in 1950, before the important Brown decision. And then he was devastated when his wife, Buster, died in 1955 after an illness during which Thurgood stopped all of his work to take care of her.

A few years later one of the justices said that the Brown decision was probably "the most important decision in the history of the court."

Marshall, during his career, stood before the nine justices of the Supreme Court to argue thirty-two cases. Of these, twenty-nine were decided in his favor!

By 1959 people all over the world were calling Thurgood Marshall "Mr. Civil Rights."

In 1960, Thurgood Marshall was invited to work on writing a constitution for Kenya, which was to become an independent republic. He traveled to England and to Kenya to help draft the constitution, which included safeguards for the rights of the white people who were a minority in Kenya. In the early 1960s, Marshall made several visits to Africa, including a visit to Kenya for their independence celebration.

President John F. Kennedy nominated Marshall in 1961 to be a judge on the U.S. Second Circuit Court of Appeals. During his tenure as a circuit court judge, he made 112 rulings, all of which were later upheld by the Supreme Court.

In 1965, President Lyndon Johnson appointed Marshall to be the U.S. solicitor general, the lawyer who represents the

United States before the Supreme Court. Thurgood's second wife, Cecelia Suyat, whom he had married in 1956, and their two young sons, Thurgood Jr. and John, were present to watch Marshall being sworn in as the thirty-third solicitor general of the United States, and the first African-American to hold this post.

Many were surprised that Marshall accepted this position. He was giving up a lifetime appointment as a judge, while the post of solicitor general could be ended at any time. Also in this role he would be arguing cases for the government. He did not mind that the job was not lifetime, and he felt that he was still defending justice for the people and their rights as stated in the Constitution and its amendments.

Just two years later, in 1967, President Lyndon Johnson named Thurgood Marshall to be an associate justice of the Supreme Court of the United States! He was the first

African-American to be a Supreme Court justice.

Justice Thurgood Marshall served on the court for twenty-four years, finally retiring in 1991 due to ill health. He voted with the court on many important decisions through the years. He died in 1993.

Throughout his lifetime, Justice Thurgood Marshall was a fighter through the legal justice system for the rights of his fellow men. His conviction was strong and true that the right and just interpretation of the Constitution and its amendments should provide equal protection under the law for all Americans!